ANGUS PETER CAMPBELL has been described as the Mark Twain of modern Gaelic literature. He has won many awards for his writing, including the Bardic Crown and a Creative Scotland Award, and starred in the acclaimed Gaelic film *Seachd: The Inaccessible Pinnacle*. He was born and brought up on the Island of South Uist. He now lives at Reul-na-maidne with his wife and children. *Archie and the North Wind* is his first novel in English.

Archie and the North Wind

ANGUS PETER CAMPBELL

Luath Press Limited

EDINBURGH

www.luath.co.uk

First published 2010

ISBN: 978-1-906817-38-1

The publisher acknowledges the support of

towards the publication of this volume.

The paper used in this book is recyclable. It is elemental chlorine free (ECF) and manufactured from sustainable wood pulp forests. This paper and its manufacture are approved by the National Association of Paper Merchants (NAPM), working towards a more sustainable future.

Printed and bound by Thomson Litho, East Kilbride

Typeset in 11 point Sabon

Drawing of Gobhlachan by Liondsaidh Chaimbeul

A' cuimhneachadh R. agus sluagh na sgeòil
Remembering R. and the workers in the wind

Acknowledgments

Le taing do Chailean MacIlleathain bhon a chuala mi sgeulachd bheag Eairdsidh an toiseach. My thanks to Cailean Maclean who first told me the joke about Archie.

'The Wee White Bull', as told by Betsy Whyte, Montrose, to Barbara McDermitt, transcribed in *Tocher* 54 and 55; I translated the original Scots story into Gaelic and then 're-translated' these into Gobhlachan's English. Thanks for permission to reproduce these stories to Dr Cathlin Macaulay, Archivist, and Dr Margaret MacKay, Director, School of Scottish Studies.

'Hector and the Balloon', as recorded from Angus MacLennan, Frobost, South Uist, on 30 April 1958, by John Lorne Campbell. This extract from *Stories from South Uist* by Angus MacLellan, translated by John Lorne Campbell, is reproduced by permission of Birlinn Ltd, www.birlinn.co.uk. Thanks also to Magda Sagarsuza at the Canna Archive, and the National Trust for Scotland.

'The Red Book', 'Connal's Tale', 'Hurrah for Kintail' and 'The King of Lochlann's Three Daughters' can all be found in J.F. Campbell's great nineteenth century collection, *Popular Tales of the West Highlands*, gathered from carters, servant-girls, fishermen, nursemaids, drovers, tinkers, shoemakers, blind fiddlers and others.

The little story about the snowball and the rabbits (in a different form) from Eòghainn MacKinnon, Elgol, Isle of Skye.

Thanks to my wife, Liondsaidh Chaimbeul, for the cover drawing and for the picture of Gobhlachan, to Pàdraig Tarscabhaig for technical help, to Jennie Renton for her sensitive editing, and to the excellent team at Luath Press for all their support and encouragement – Gavin MacDougall, Leila Cruickshank, Tom Bee, Christine Wilson and Nina Haese.

I

THE OLD STORY has it that Archie, tired of the north wind, sought to extinguish it.

He built a house, then a wall, then a doubling-wall, and fences and hedge-barriers, but the whining whistle of the winter wind still filtered through. The more he refused to listen, the louder it roared.

So he planted a forest to the north side, then dug deep to establish a lake to absorb some of the wind's force, then another thick forest on the far side, but as he lay in bed on those long January nights he could hear the whole world move.

'Was that a sparrow, somewhere to the north?'

'Impossible, in the depth of winter.'

'Maybe it was to the south, with the swirling gale carrying it through the barriers? To sound as if it was coming from the north?'

He looked out the attic window where the universe was quiet and white in the snow.

Lying back in bed he listened again. The sound of breathing downstairs, where his wife rested. The distant throb of a television in his son's bedroom. How loudly the snowflakes fell onto his window. He was a thin man. Like a wisp of grass really, all short and stubbly in the winter, lush and long in the summer. Where sheep grazed, and cows munched and the *speal* – the scythe – mowed. How precious grass is in this bare, rocky place.

Years ago, in a Geography book in school, he was told that the snow came from the east. Born in Siberia, it travelled across Russia like an army, recruiting flakes to fall gently on these western shores as a soft blanket on a bed, pure and pristine and white. Virginal they called it then, which now seemed such an archaic word in a world where everyone was born knowing.

And then the thaw would come and the white world grew ugly, messing up the streets and muddying the socks inside the shoes until all the snowmen had gone, leaving only a fractured stick here, a disused scarf there.

When he was born, Archie knew nothing. Slowly he realised that the sweet thing in his mouth was his mother, and that the dark thing that hid the world from him was the inside of a drawer in which he slept, and that the stranger who came home from sea every year-and-a-half was called his father.

When he was five he was sent to school and was told that other worlds existed beyond the fank and the hill and the shoreline. They had different colours from the one he inhabited. An elongated green one was called Canada, while the Union of Soviet Socialist Republics was red and the United States of America light blue, just like the sky on a bright summer's day.

His republic was divided into quarterly segments, called *earrach* and *samhradh* and *foghar* and *geamhradh* – spring and summer and autumn and winter, though the old people never tired of telling him that these were modern divisions which made no sense to them, who calculated by the old dispensations beyond the Gregorian calendar.

'In our days,' they would say, 'we measured differently. By the moon and stars and the sun and tide.' And they would chant out old names to him, which made as much sense as saying Pluto or Mars or Saturn – names which he had once detected on an atlas hidden in the teacher's room, tucked behind the blueish globe.

And they would patiently explain to him how February really began in what was now January and never finished until what he called March was almost done, and how April used to be in two parts, pre-sowing and post-sowing, and how August was the month of both the harvest and the badger moon, and how *Samhain* marked the beginning of winter, which would always be long and wet if it happened to fall on a Wednesday. Most of his life these remained glorious truths as well as mysteries, like the name Tanganyika which he recalled from the story of David Livingstone, and the name Aix-la-Chapelle which he remembered from the war stories of his uncle, his father's brother, who returned with one leg and one shiny medal from a muddy place called France.

Archie himself was no hero. He had never done much, neither college nor university. Leaving school at fourteen he had been apprenticed to the local smithy, a wizened old man reduced to the nickname 'Gobhlachan' – literally, 'Crotch-ridden'. Some said this was merely because he always sat astride his anvil like a horseman, others alluded to withered balls; some argued through age, others through natural disposition, some seeming to recall an accident of long ago when his testicles were crushed by the back-kick of a Clydesdale horse he was shoeing out in the open yard.

Whichever it was, Gobhlachan's trade was a dying art. In the twinkling of an eye, all the horses were gone and the little work he procured was a mixture of welding for the emerging cars and the re-moulding of iron railings for garden furniture.

Archie was taken on as an apprentice in a golden moment, when a woman from Poland arrived in the area with a string of horses, intending to open a beach riding school down by the shoreline. The woman – Olga Swirszczynska – had once been a ballet teacher and musician, but a back injury – caused in an air accident, she claimed – had finished her career and forced her to try all kinds of exercises, from yoga to gentle horse-riding, in an effort at regaining fluidity.

Instead, she fell in love with horses: their smell and physical presence, their power and beauty, their raggedness and temper, their sheer hard-earned intimacy. Sure, there were some who nuzzled up and cooried near like well-behaved children, but these were never the best: when put to the test out in the dawn air, they were too soft and lazy.

It was always those other ones – the awkward bastards whose trust had to be earned – who proved best when the rain hammered down at five a.m. and you led them leaping over the down hedges.

That was in England, of course, before the stable failed and went bankrupt and before she moved north, picking up horses here, there and everywhere on the way, from dealers and circuses, from farmyards and the RSPCA, finally arriving in this godforsaken, windy spot on a cold April morning when the Atlantic was brewing like a kettle, preparing for the storm that went down in history as *An Siabadh Mòr*, The Great Shaking.

Those who lived through it described it as you would describe the moon: as a marvel placed above your garden. 'It came,' they said, 'unexpectedly, from the north, though the sea had been thrashing in from the west all night. By that time, everything was tilting eastwards – the haystacks and the peatstacks and the carts and byres – but just when we thought it was all over, it suddenly moved northwards and the icy wind blew as if you could see God's cheeks bellowing in and out, and it left nothing standing. We survived because we hid, in the hollows burrowed out in the machairs where the little-people once lived, though the bones we shared the hollows with are now all gone, taken by the later storms and the erosion.'

Naturally, of course, some folk blamed the strange Polish woman, who had arrived that very day with her string of horses. 'How did she survive anyway?' they muttered, not really believing that the horses had corralled themselves into a magic circle round the woman, nose to tail, their shiny flanks offering her all the world's protection from the hurricane.

Once the wind abated, this was the first sound the survivors heard: the thunderous roar of the hooves on the hardened machair as the horses ran southwards, away from the cradle of the remembered storm. She herself arrived later, on foot, dressed in man's clothing – something unheard of in the district except in the sailors' tales of women in far-off lands who wore turbans on their heads and wielded scimitars as wildly as the Turks.

By that time the horses were subdued and grazing on the seaweed-strewn thin grass. They snorted and neighed quietly when she came in sight, continuing their slow munching as if nothing had ever happened except this eternal chewing, here, in this stubbly sand, on the very edge of the world.

When the woman came to Gobhlachan, the talk was inevitable: the strange horsewoman and the unballed man. What a fine match they would make, she with her long wild hair and he with his small, sharp claws. The meeting of fire with earth, or of '*òrd le ighne*', hammer with anvil, as they named it.

In actual fact, despite their physical differences, Olga Swirszczynska and Gobhlachan were the perfect match. Not so much fire with earth or hammer to anvil, as hand to glove and swan to lake. They were gentle with other, like wild horses tamed, or like sheared sheep.

'Of course, he's the woman,' the men sneered enviously, watching Olga each morning as she harnessed the horses, tethered the ploughs to their haunches then set off to furrow the ancient fields between the two rivers which had lain unused for generations. And she would be seen in the thin dawn light leading her horses through the phosphorescence down to the seashore, where they could be glimpsed moving through the misty binoculars like ghosts in an old story.

She did all the work which had hitherto belonged to men, from peat-cutting to thatching the byres, from line-fishing to burying the horses when they died.

'*Chaidh an tarbh beag a' spothadh*,' they said of Gobhlachan – 'The small bull has been truly castrated' – though he was as happy as Fionn the Warrior resting on the Hill of Plenty and continued daily to sit astride his anvil, a cup of tea in one hand and in the other a hammer, which he regularly rattled against the iron, imagining the sparks flying as in the believed olden days.

But none of this had happened when Archie was first taken on as Gobhlachan's apprentice, for at that time Olga had just arrived in the district. Once the storm had ceased, much repair work needed to be done and Gobhlachan's services were required everywhere, to fix broken axles and wheels and carts and bits-and-bobs for which Archie had no name but which were essential for survival, from the small chain which hooked the pot to the fire to the anchor-hooks which held the boats fast against the tide.

The day he was fourteen he left school forever, as he was legally entitled to do. 'The law has its uses,' the schoolmaster said to him when the bell rang for the last time.

It was now Monday. Instead of lying in bed as usual till sunrise, he rose while the sickle moon still slept in the sky. Instead of the woollen school clothing, he put on his dungarees and wellingtons and went outside where the arc of his urine perfectly reversed the sickle of the lying moon.

He smelt the air, which was frosty and sweet, a mixture of rain and manure, and looked up at the expanse of the skies where the stars were twinkling in all their beauty. The Great Bear dancing to the north, dragging the Plough behind him. What an eternal job, with Andromeda sparkling high to the south like a cran of herring flung into the skies.

He went into the byre, where the cows snorted smoke into the air. Their dull eyes looked at him, knowing that it was still the middle of the night, and they lay their heads down again in the straw, waiting for the real dawn and the cockerel's call which would come at the proper time.

Archie went back outside, suddenly realising that this was it: his life was to be made here, between the byre and the shore, between The Great Bear and Andromeda. He thought of that place – that institution – he'd been in for the past nine years: the school, and what it had all meant. A hot lunch each day – broth – and lots of things told him by the one teacher, which sounded magnificent, but made little sense.

How Richard the Lionheart – what a hero he was! – had conquered Jerusalem and tamed Saladin and had had his heart taken across Europe after his death by a singer called Blonden who had found his body abandoned in the Forest of Rouen. At least, that was the version Archie heard, well before the later versions emerged depicting The Lionheart as an unfaithful homosexual war criminal.

Like leaves of a book, the two things which lay before him were the land and the sea. The earth, from which came the few things which sustained life – potatoes and sheep and cattle – and the sea, from which came the sweet things – herring and cod and saithe and lythe, as well as death.

They were married, of course, the earth and the sea. Mating like the bull and the cow, which he'd seen so often in the rocky fields. The cow bellowing for days and then the bull rising high and thrusting that stiff red thing inside as they slithered forwards in the drizzly mist.

Without the sea the earth was dry and barren, and that morning he could see the spindrift wooing the earth, spraying it with its salty mist. Archie walked down through the winter fields to the edge of the machair, where the mating was remorseless, the huge Atlantic waves thrashing on to the shore, the beach strewn with the debris of the thrusts – tangle and seaweed and nets and bottles and fragments of broken timber.

This was no division between land and sea: such a choice was unimaginable. To survive on land was to rely on the sea, and Archie had long known that his adult life would begin here, gathering the sea's jewels to fertilise the land for the spring sowing. So as the sun rose low to the east above Ben Mòr, he bowed to the task, back to the Atlantic wind.

'Never wear gloves,' had been the chant since childhood, 'they make your hands soft.' So Archie bent into the seaweed, striking at its roots with the curved sickle in his bare hands, beginning to build up the first real heap of his life. The heap which would grow and lengthen, then be carried inland on his back in a creel and spread thin on the ground out of which emerged the potato in early autumn.

But the real work was the tangle, each root like snatching

a hair out of the giant's head. The story was that the sea was merely the sky for the *Fuamhaire Mòr* – the Great Giant – who had been exiled beneath the waves for once having touched the sky above with his outstretched arms. The full story was that when the earth heaved into shape, dividing itself into continents, it rose up in giant form and stretched itself its full length, the fingertips which subsequently became China and America inadvertently touching the sky where the gods dwelt, disturbing their slumber.

In their anger, the giant was exiled back down to the bottom of the ocean, and as he fell from the sky back into the sea huge lumps fell off him which – of course – became the earth as we know it today, melted and moulded and forged by time and heat and tide.

'The giant's arse,' they say, when someone mentions England.

'His toe,' when Italy is displayed.

'A snot from his nose,' when they see Iceland.

Though, of course, the giant's parts are all moveable, depending on time and place and tribe and prejudice.

Archie knew all that to be nonsense, though that knowledge did not diminish the myth. The sea's power was evident whether a giant stayed beneath it or not. The sky's infinity was obvious despite the blue school globe which contained it all. The Earth's ultimate willingness to be harvested, in spite of the frost and the blight and the hard soil, was proven year after year. Archie knew that life had always been a contest with the giant, and that to pluck a single hair from his head, or yield a corner of his toenail away, was a constant triumph.

But the cold! To sink hands into the freezing sea-water each morning, time and again, lifting the dripping stocks round your wrists. And the fumbling for the pen-knife and the hacking away, leaving the bare stalk which you split with both hands as if you were indeed the giant, separating main from main on your plunge into the freezing waters.

Again and again and again, breaking the stalks, one after the other, each winter morning. The 1st of January, bitterly cold with a north-easterly. The 2nd of January, equally cold with a stronger wind from the north. The 3rd of January, hailstones sweeping in from the north-east, hammering against the soaking oilskins. The 4th of January, real snow falling on the sand; and on it went, forever, ceaselessly, as Archie walked down to the shore each morning, head bent into the wind, to his appointed task.

By the beginning of April the giant's arm was bent. Archie had accumulated about a quarter-of-a-mile's worth of tangle, stretching in a thin line above a row of barrels carried from the disused fish-curing factory which had closed before the last great war. The seaweed itself had already been spread on the fields, but the tangle was the magic profit margin: one of the few sources of surplus income available to an unskilled boy.

On the first Monday after Easter the boat would arrive and take the tangle southwards, in exchange for money. 'You'll get £5 for that,' some of the other lads said, though Archie kept his mouth shut and listened to the older men who mentioned much higher sums – £20, £30, even £40.

John the Goblin – so-called because of his weakened leg – hirpled into view one day and sat down, rolling a cigarette. 'Do you know something?' said John the Goblin. 'That stuff,' – pointing to the tangle – 'is used to make French letters.' He inhaled his cigarette. 'Just think of that. Stalks for stalks, eh?'

Archie had no idea what he was talking about. 'Also,' continued John the Goblin, 'they use it to make toothpaste and hair spray and fireworks and cannons.' He spat out fragments of tobacco. 'Makes you think, doesn't it? Almost makes you think, eh? Would you like a fag?'

'Sure,' said Archie; and there, sheltering behind the tangle-bank from the gusting wind, clumsily rolled his first cigarette, taking five goes at lighting it in the face of the swirling breeze. Finally, huddled beneath his jacket, the paper caught light and the glow was like the glow of his granny's tilley lamp in the early evening, signalling warmth and pleasure and a long night of stories.

Inevitably, he coughed at the first rough draw of nicotine, but John the Goblin merely smiled, saying, 'It happens to all of us at the beginning. But by the time you've finished it, you can't get enough of it.' And it was true. So the Goblin divided his shredded tobacco in two, saying, 'We'll go halfers. And I'll get you a proper tin later, to make a real man of you.' He smiled. 'Of course, you'll need to pay me. A stalk for a stalk, as they say. What about going halfers on the tangle? Half the tangle for as much tobacco as I can supply?'

'I'm not half as daft as I look,' said Archie. 'Why don't I just buy my own tobacco?'

The Goblin laughed. 'Aye! And where? Where do you think I get mine? Do you think I just wander out to that shitty shop at the pier to buy their overpriced rubbish? No way, José.'

The pier shop was the only shop in the place. That mythic establishment where you could buy everything from a needle to an anchor.

'And if you did buy it, it's like smoking horse-shit,' said the Goblin. 'God only knows where he gets that rubbish from. If I were you, I would just crush that tangle down and smoke it instead.'

'So where do you get your stuff from?' Archie asked.

'Ah, but that's a trade secret,' smiled the Goblin, tapping his nose. 'That's what you would pay half your tangle for.' He rolled another cigarette, lit it, and handed it to Archie. 'Think about it,' he said. 'As you bend into that wind cutting the tangle, wouldn't it be nice to look forward to a really good smoke every hour or so? Just you think about it!' And John the Goblin hirpled off across the sand dunes, the tin in his back pocket glinting in the watery sunlight.

That turned out to be the actual day of *An Siabadh Mòr,* The Great Shaking. No sooner had John the Goblin disappeared out of sight beyond the sand dunes than the wind began to rise, shaking the very barrels on which Archie's future rested. Behind him the sea began to boil, and to the west and north the sky turned dark purple as if someone in the heavens had spilt an inkwell. Archie immediately regretted not having accepted the Goblin's offer. A fag would be great consolation now. It would give him time to think, as he huddled beneath the barrels, rolling it slowly. Instead, there was one less thing between himself and eternity. For not having a cigarette he was barer, more at the mercy of the coming storm.

He hardly got home before the wind was at its full hurricane strength. For the first time in his life his abject poverty was an advantage. Too poor to have ever moved beyond a blackhouse, the family's low-lying stone house was their salvation. More underground than overground, they were like beavers huddled in the darkness beneath the chaos. They heard the wind, but were physically untouched by it. As objects flew by outside, Archie and his parents and brothers and sisters and aged aunt sat on stools round the fire, conscious of the need to be silent.

Death, they all knew, was outside, so this was no time for tea or scones or idle chat. Each sat quiet, listening to the great storm raging, knowing that this time round it would not call for them. They all remembered the old stories they'd heard, of how Death always came in disguise. The Grim Reaper was, of course, a joke, for who could be frightened of one so familiar as he travelled through the villages in his grey cloak and with his shining scythe over his shoulder? They had seen him so often that he seemed a permanent inhabitant with his own croft and boat, his own potatoes and milk. He even tipped his cap at them.

But the man was a master of disguises, according to the old people, and could turn himself into any shape or form, animate or inanimate. What else were the rocks against which the fowlers had fallen for all these years? Or the sea, into which so many had fallen, drowned? Or the Fever, which came as a yellow-spotted guest from the visiting ship which had called all these years ago?

'He was beautiful,' one old woman was heard to say, 'when he came ashore. You should have seen him, swimming towards us in a yellow polka-dot bathing suit, glinting in the noonday sun. By evening, all the young people in the village had a raging temperature with their skins erupting all over with yellow spots. By morning, none of them were alive. And that's the strange thing, the Fever didn't affect anyone over the age of twelve. They were all buried in shrouds which turned yellow as soon as they touched the corpses. *Am Galar Mòr Buidhe*, The Great Yellow Fever we called it, on account of the shrouds.'

And the yellow-shrouded one was all-blowing outside, for all his strength. They could hear his lungs wheezing as he ran through the air, his heart beating strongly as he pounded against the stone, his tongue and fingers and toes and tail trying to squeeze in through each tiny chink which disfigured the crumbling stonework keeping him at bay.

Why didn't we repair that tiny section by the window while we had the chance? they all thought, as they watched his sharp fingernail easing through the miniscule hole which they had all ignored too long. Archie moved to crumple an old cut of tweed into a ball which he stuffed into the small hole, crushing his fingernail.

They all listened as he raged outside, roaring with anger as he flung the universe to shreds. He breathed down through the chimney, adding black billows of smoke to the darkness. His nostrils smelt of peat as he crawled through the house, suffocating them. He was all wind and rain and hail and snow. He was rock and sea and river and bog. He was famine and hunger and sickness and poverty. He was sun and moon and light and stars. A family member and a terrible stranger.

Grandfather, taken in the broad light of day as he lay resting in the shade of the sun in his homemade wicker basket. Joanna, stricken down in the height of her youth, the morning of the day before her wedding. She had been trying on her bridal gown when the headache came, soft and dull and throbbing, as if he'd rolled himself into a spark of perfume turned sour, a great sweetness gone rancid.

I remember the man's watch, Archie's father thought. It was marked one minute after mid-day. And the sun was shining in all its glory, even through the smoke and fire and carnage.

'Did you say something?' Granny asked.

'The Somme,' Archie's father answered. 'July 1916. A bright summer's day. A head flew past me. I thought it was a football, at first. Rags of flesh fell on me and when I looked down, this severed hand lay beside me with the pocket watch still held firm in the grip of the hand. He must have been an officer, for they were the only ones who carried timepieces. He must have been checking for the next advance.'

Maybe it was a minute past midnight, Archie thought. As if that made any difference.

'And they tell me that snowdrops and pansies now grow there, as if nothing ever happened. Donald-John was there a year ago and he says it's now like a meadow, with proper gravestones at the end and plaques and markers and signposts and tourist information, with bees buzzing round the clover the day he was there. He even brought back a pot of honey which tasted as sweet as our own potatoes when mashed with milk.'

And suddenly it was all quiet outside, as if the Somme Meadow had been rolled out, already bursting with clover.

'He's gone,' muttered Granny, beginning once again to stir the pot which hung from an iron hook above the open fire. The sweet smell of soup filled the air, as if all the taste buds had been re-awakened, and Archie's mother returned to kneading the bread on the long wooden table, raising up a storm cloud of flour about the room.

Archie and his father went outside to survey the damage. All was still. Not a breath of wind in the air. Not a single cloud in the sky. The sea electric blue on the horizon. All the winter hayricks in the village had been swept away. Not a single cart remained on its wheels. All the houses were roofless. Rocks which hadn't moved since the creation of the world were gone. The entire landscape was translated, as if a giant's hand had swept across the district, flattening raised things, lowering exalted things, moving immovable things. The hills, of course, remained, as did the river and the fields and the lochs. What had changed was the human landscape: people's houses and byres and possessions, all swept away.

It was only afterwards that the real cost was counted, when funeral after funeral took place, each one paying his due to the great visitor.

Archie's tangle was destroyed along with all other things. When he walked down to the shore in the evening stillness, it was as if he had never been there before, as if he had never spent these frozen morning hacking away at the stalks in the pre-dawn light, as if he had never – stoically and patiently – build up his great wall of tangle, single stalk by single stalk, to the quarter-mile length which had tempted John the Goblin along with his sweet weed, the taste of which Archie could still feel in the back of his mouth and nostrils, and now all gone like a dream overtaken by the morning light.

That was the day Gobhlachan came into his own. All things were broken, and the wizened man with the crushed balls was the only one in the area who could repair them. He had the anvil and the bellows, the fire and the tongs. A succession of widows and orphans made their way to him, carrying the remnants of a plough or of a kettle or of a cart and leaving them in separate bundles by his forge door.

There was so much destruction that Gobhlachan sent word for help and Archie was the first to call by.

'Don't worry, boy,' Gobhlachan immediately said to him. 'That Goblin isn't the only one around here who can lay his paws on good tobacco.' And he lit his pipe, handing it to Archie, who puffed and coughed and drew in the sweet nicotine. 'And I won't charge you half your tangle either,' added Gobhlachan. 'In fact, I won't charge you any tangle at all. In fact, you will never have to go back to your tangle again. Plenty work here, son, if you want it. Hard work. Warm work. Right here by the fire.'

And he beckoned Archie over, telling him to lift the stoking shovel which lay by the oven door. And there, by the forge door, Archie learned all there was to learn about iron. How soft and fluid and watery it really was before it was plunged into the flames. How you could shape it into any form you wished – curved, opaque, translucent, hard, soft, thick, thin. How fast you had to be to control it, before it assumed a shape you had never desired or imagined. How impossible it was to reverse the curve or the fault or the crack once it hardened or set. Creation was irreparable.

The amount which ended up on the scrapheap! Hooves which turned out like bits of turd, shapeless pans, kettles which could not hold a thing, parts of ploughs which were as useless as a star on a summer's day. But all that – that physical stuff – was the least of it. Gobhlachan's lore was what really mattered: stories and trade secrets which were as fluid, or as set, as the iron itself. How iron protected you from the Fairies and safeguarded you from the dead. How a nail above the lintel of the door ensured that no evil ever entered; how a reaping-hook placed beneath the bed was a surefire guarantee that no mother or child died in childbirth. Gobhlachan never used the word 'magic', but that's what it was: manifold ways of avoiding death and misfortune.

Iron itself was, of course, magical. With hooves, your steeds ran faster, across all kinds of terrain, than anyone else's horses. With a reaping hook you harvested bread. With an iron plough you eased the goodness out of the earth. With keys you locked – and opened – chests. With swords you conquered. With a gun barrel you triumphed. With a knife you could skin and dismember the deer.

Gobhlachan had other, even more fantastic stories. How the Devil had tried to marry the most beautiful girl on the island. The time another Archie swam backwards up the Niagara Falls, watched by his rival. Why beggars were called Pilgrims of the Mist. How Donald was tamed by whisky in the well. How women made clay effigies. How you could travel all the way to America on a single wisp of straw. Transformation was everywhere. He said:

Long ago, there lived a king and queen and they had five lovely sons. Then late in life they had this wee daughter. And she was beautiful. And they all adored her. Every one of them, the boys and the king and the queen. And they were all so happy. And the boys used to take her out to play, you see, because there was a big meadow and parks and trees that led down to the water. And they had ample place to play.

So the mother says, 'Mind you look after your wee sister now.'

'Oh, yes, we'll look after her, Mother.'

But you know what boys are. They like to climb trees and play with bows and arrows and things like that. So they would leave her – she was very young, you see – and tell her to sit and make daisy chains or something in the meadow while they rampaged through the woods.

But one day she's sitting there trying to make daisy chains, when this white bull came making circles round about her. Wide circles at first. But every time it went round, it came closer and closer, you see.

And it says, 'Hello.'

And she says, 'Oh, hello.'

And the wee white bull says, 'Why are you sitting there on your own?'

'The boys are away playing,' she says. 'They're coming back for me soon.'

He says, 'Now, wouldn't you like to have some fun as well as the boys?'

'Oh yes.'

'Well, come on. You jump on my back and we can have a nice run around the meadow and you'll love it.'

'Oh no, no, I don't think so,' she says. 'Oh, I'm frightened to go on your back. You're too big.'

'I'm not really big,' the bull says. 'And anyway, I'll kneel down and then you can get on my back,' he says. 'You'll love it. Come on.'

And after a while he persuades her – circling round about her in that way, he sort of mesmerised her, you see.

She says, 'All right.'

So the bull kneels down, this white bull. And she got gets his back as he says, 'Now hold on to my horns.'

She held on to the horns, but this bull took off with her. And it kept going and it kept going until it came to the shore. It was then that the boys noticed. And they ran and ran, thinking they would catch it, because they never thought it would go into the water, you see. But it did go into the water and it kept going into the water and it kept going. And she's holding on to the horns and shouting, 'Let me down, let me down, let me down.'

And this bull says, 'No, you're not getting down.'

And these boys, when they finally reached to the shore, the last thing they saw was their sister and the bull disappearing over the horizon, over the water. So they were terrified to go home and tell their father and their mother. But they just had to. So the king and the queen were absolutely hysterical about their wee lassie – and so were the boys. They all just loved her.

The king was getting on a bit by this time, you see, quite unable to go in search for her. So the three oldest boys, they say, 'Look, Father, we'll go and we'll get her.'

And the oldest one, his name was Jack, he says, 'I'll not come back, Father, until I get her. I promise you that.'

So off the boys went.

Now they had been well taught with swordsmanship and all the things boys were taught at that time, you see. So they took their swords and things with them and away they went.

And they went from one place to another, from one place to another, till their money went down and their feet were sore with walking. The horses were worn out. They had to give them up. And they started walking and walking and their feet were terribly sore. Their hair was growing long. Now and then they would stop and have a shave in some old body's house, because they would ask any old person if they needed wood chopped or whatever and get a wee bit of food and a bed for themselves in exchange, you see.

And this went on for years until the younger son says, 'This is no use. We're never going to find her. We may as well face the fact,' he says. 'I'm going home.'

So his brother Jack says, 'Well, please yourself. I don't blame you.'

So the younger one he went away home.

And the other two kept going on and on and on, across ferries and across water and into different countries and all over. But no word could they get of the bull or their sister.

Until the second oldest one, he says, 'It's no use, Jack, I'm going home too.'

Well, Jack says, 'I'm keeping going on. I promised to go on till I found her. I'm going to do just that.'

So the second-oldest laddie, he went away home to his father and mother with the sad news. But Jack he kept on and on and on. And every day he always found a wee bite from somebody. And one day this old henwife that he was working for, when she was giving him a bowl of porridge and that, and a cup of tea, and he was telling her his story – you see, he told everybody that he met in case someone had heard of the bull.

'No, laddie,' she says, 'I never heard nothing of a white bull or wee lassie. I never even heard mention of them no way,' she says. 'But see that mountain there?'

He says, 'Yes?'

'Well,' she says, 'up there in that mountain there's a wind trapped into a hole,' she says. 'It's trapped in there and it cannot get out. And they tell me it knows everything, no matter what you want to know, if you go up there,' she says, 'and look for a wee hole.'

And Jack says, 'If there's a hole why can he not get out?'

'No, no, no,' she says, 'I've never seen the wind. Don't you know that it can't come up through a wee hole? Just look for a hole,' she says, 'and put your mouth to the hole and shout down into it.'

So Jack goes and he climbs and he climbs and he climbs and he climbs this mountain. And it was some mountain. And he's looking all over and all over. It's a long time before he spots this wee hole.

He says, 'I wonder if that's the hole she's speaking about?' So he put his mouth to the hole and he shouts down, 'Wind, are you there?'

'Oooooooooooo.'

He says, 'Well, listen, please. I'm looking for my wee sister that was stolen by a white bull years ago. And I've been tramping and walking and swimming and rowing all over the world trying to find her. And I'm really exhausted, Wind. Please tell me what happened to her.'

Then he put his ear to the hole, you see.

And he heard this:

'Ooooooooooooooo.'

'What are you saying? I can't make you out,' he says. 'Try and speak a wee bit clearer.'

But all he could get was 'Oooo the Coo!'

He says, 'It sounds like "Follow the coo." Is it "Follow the coo?"'

And he put his ear again to the hole. But there was no answer.

'Ah,' he says, 'I'm off my head to listen to that silly old woman to take that road up this huge mountain and that silly wind that doesn't know anything. All I could make out was "Follow the coo, follow the coo."' He says to himself, 'What coo isn't he speaking about?' So he trudged down the mountain again. Hours and hours and hours it took him to trudge down. But when he got to the bottom, sure enough there was a cow. And this cow started to walk on. It was a-standin grazing when he came down. But it started to walk away, you see.

So Jack says, 'Well, no harm done,' he says. 'I'll follow it anyway. I'm sure that's what that wind was saying: "Follow the coo."'

So he walked after this cow and he walked after this cow for about two days. Till this cow stopped to eat the grass again, you see. And it ate away and it ate away and he's standing looking at it and going round about it. And then the cow sat down and stared chewing the cud. And Jack he sat down too beside it, you see. And suddenly he heard this voice saying, 'You might go and get me a drink of water.' And he looked round. This was the cow speaking to him.

'Oh,' he says, 'you can speak.'

'Of course I can speak,' she says. 'Go and look over there,' she says. 'There must be water beside those rushes and things over there.'

He says, 'I could do with a drink myself.' So over he goes. And he's looking about for something to carry water in, you see. And he's kicking away the grass. And he takes his sword and he's cutting down these rushes and things when this head comes, this huge beast, like a dragon, a great big mouthful of teeth. And he jumps back, terrified. And looking past in a cave – this dragon was in a cave – he sees this girl at the back of it.

And he says, 'My sister! I'll bet it's my sister!' But he's too terrified to stand and look too much. And he goes back to the cow and says, 'Oh no, no, no, you'll get no drink of water here, neither me nor you. There's a beast there and I never saw the like of him in my life,' he says. 'I've heard about dragons and that's what it must be.'

'Well,' the cow says, 'you're a big young man with a sword in your hand. Are you afraid of a beast?'

'You never saw the beast,' he says. 'It's forty times the size of you.'

'Away you go,' she says, 'Go on,' she says, 'laddie, go and kill the beast.'

'Kill the beast?' he says. 'How am I going to kill a beast like that?'

She says, 'Well, I'll tell you what to do. When it opens its mouth, you jump into its mouth, and keep well back into its mouth so that it will not be able to get its mouth closed,' she says, 'and just cut the windpipe with your sword.'

So she gave Jack heartening, you see. So down he goes and sure enough this beast opens its jaws and he jumps inside the jaws and right enough he was so far back into its gullet, it couldn't get its mouth shut. And he starts to hack and hack and hack and hack with his sword till all the windpipe is cut and the head slumps down. And he jumps out before the teeth could get him, you see. And when he looks into this cave, he says, 'No, that's not my sister.'

But the girl runs to him. She's that happy she clings on to him.

And she says, 'You don't look very pleased to have come and rescued me.'

'Well,' he says, 'I'm really looking for my sister.'

'What happened to your sister?'

'She was stolen away by a white bull,' he says, 'I can't remember how many years ago. And we've never seen nor heard of her since.'

'Well, that's what happened to me,' she says. 'But I wouldn't behave myself. Every chance I got I was running away.' And she says, 'If that's what's happened to your sister, she's probably in the same place I have been in. This is my punishment, out here with this beast, for what I have done. I just wouldn't stay, I was always trying to get away. Lots of girls try to get away and they're badly punished for it.'

And he says, 'Do you think that my sister could be there?'

'Well,' she says, 'if she's living, that's likely where she'll be. But you must take care. There's a great fortress built,' she says, 'and an army of men you've never seen the like of. There's no way you're going to get in there. I'm warning you, if you go in there you're going to your death.'

'Well,' he says, 'if I'm going to my death, I'm going to my death. 'Cause I promised I wouldn't come back without her anyway. And I'd be as well dead as wandering about this way for years and years and years.'

But anyway, he came back and he took the lassie with him. And they sat down and leaned against this cow, because she was sitting chewing the cud, you see. And the cow says, 'She's not your sister then?'

'No,' he says, 'She's not my sister. But she's somebody's bairn for all that.'

She says, 'Aye!'

And Jack says, 'She thinks my sister might be there. But there's no way I'll get her out,' he says. 'It's a king that changes himself into a bull and goes and steals these bairns and lassies.'

And the cow says, 'What do you mean, no way?'

'Well, he has an army of thousands.'

'But,' says the cow, 'you can have an army of thousands too, if you just listen to me. I'll tell you what to do,' she says. 'Go with your sword to the dragon's head and cut the gums away and pull every tooth out that you can get.'

He says, 'Ah, there are thousands.'

'Well,' she says, 'Pull them. And get the lassie to help. Go on, you, and give him a hand,' she says. 'Now go and do what I'm telling you.'

'Might as well,' he says.

But they got a drink of water anyway. The well was free now, you see, with no beast guarding it. So having this lassie, they pulled and pulled and they pulled and they pulled and he yanked and he cut and the lassie pulled them out and threw them in a heap, all these teeth.

And he went back to the cow. He says, 'What am I going to do with that now?'

She says, 'I'll tell you. You're going to stick them in the ground all round about you.'

'Ah me,' he says, 'I must be mad listening to a cow, but I'll do it anyway.'

So him and the lassie both, they stuck all these teeth and they kept sticking and sticking until it was pitch dark night and they couldn't see to stick any more.

And the cow says, 'Ah, that should do you,' she says. 'Go on and lie down and get a wee rest to yourselves.'

Jack says, 'Aw, it's all right for you lying there chewing the cud, but we never had a bite to eat. I know I never had a bite since yesterday – the meat I got from that old henwife.'

'Ach,' says the cow, 'never mind, son. Put your hand in my ear, you'll get plenty to eat.' So he put his hand in the cow's ear and sure enough this meat came up in front of him, and him and this lassie sat and ate. And then they slept up against the cow's side.

So when Jack woke in the morning he gave himself a stretch and blinked his eyes like that and he looked round about him, there's all this lying round about him. 'What in the name of God is that?' he says.

And he got up and he went and looked round about. And you know what it was? Men with armour, gold armour and they were in all stages. Some of them hadn't their heads up out of the ground; some of them right up out of the ground; some of them as far as he could see round about him. They were all coming up, all these men.

And the cow says, 'Aye,' she says, 'that's your army. Now go and see if you can get your sister.'

So he got all these soldiers. And he had some idea what to do, being a king's son, you see. So he led the army to this fortress where this king lived, and sure enough it was a big strong fortress, with thousands and thousands of soldiers. But this army Jack had, he never heard or saw fighters like them. And he went in there and there was a great battle and he beat them. And he rushed in and got this king. And he got hold of him and he tarred him and feathered him, he put a match to him and he says, 'The world's well rid of you. I have no qualms about doing this for what you've done to all these bairns and wee lassies and things.'

And sure enough, he found his sister. She recognised him right away. And he recognised her. And he took her out and he took her back to where the cow and this other lassie were.

Now for the first time he really took a look at this other lassie, you see. And she was as bonnie as a summer's night. And he began to speak nice to her and asked her if she like to come back with him if she had no place to go now.

So he took her back and his sister back and, oh, the carry-on when they got to that castle where the mother and father was. And he married the lassie, so he brought back a wife and his sister and they lived happily ever afterwards.

Gobhlachan, of course, told the story in Gaelic and it was also, of course, a different version of the story, but this is the one Archie remembered, or thought he remembered and told or re-told or embellished a thousand and one times over the years.

He remembered Gobhlachan, sitting cross-legged astride the anvil, hammering the melting horseshoes into shape as he told of Jack and the cowardly brothers, the poor sister and the beast, the dragon and the cow. Somehow Archie knew that the actual magic was in the words themselves, not in the events. The stories were the iron, to be shaped and moulded. And as Gobhlachan hammered and smelted the fluid iron, first into a horseshoe, then into a poker, then into a gun barrel, then into a pot, then into the coulter of a plough, Archie saw that he was doing the same thing with words – turning glass into a mirror, an apple into a lake, a shoe into a boat, teeth into soldiers.

Who was this girl, he asked himself, taken away by this white bull and incarcerated against her will for so many years? And what, or who, was the bull? And the dragon, the cow, the soldiers, and that other girl rescued from the depths of the cave once the dragon was killed and his useful teeth removed?

It was at that point that Olga Swirszczynska arrived on the scene, like a woman out of one of Gobhlachan's story, wild, unkempt and foreign, with a string of horses in tow. Was she the girl, Archie asked himself, taken captive years ago and still roaming the world in search of her lost parents? Were her horses human, or at least semi-human, like the cow in the story, and what dragon or beast or king kept her within his kingdom, guarded by thousand of invisible soldiers?

She turned out to be none of these things, but exactly what she said she was – a Polish exile, a former ballet teacher and musician whose back injury had forced her to alternatives, and who had fallen in love with the ways of horses and now wished to set up a riding school here on the great white beaches that ran for ever along the very edge of the Atlantic.

Where else could be better, where the horses could run free, in this marvellous combination of wind, water and air? Where else could be better than where earth ran out and only sea remained? What better for horses than the wind in their manes, their hooves on the sand, their burning feet constantly washed by salt water as they ran and ran and ran along the perfect beach?

That too was only a version, for so many things were missed out of the story.

Archie never heard it directly from Olga herself, but over the years Gobhlachan leaked out other versions of the story, much as you would add a window to a house, exposing an extra view, or sail a different way round the island to see the cliffs, or the mountains, or the caves on the far side. These clues had to be interpreted, of course, for Gobhlachan never told anything directly, as it were – he never sailed straight up the river, but carried his canoe of words on his shoulders, paddling up through creeks and streams, taking diversions, pausing, hesitating, turning back and resting, so that you always needed a personal compass to know where you were, or might have been. You always needed a non-existent map and dictionary to work out the country you might be going to.

She'd been a revolutionary in the Uprising, and a novice nun. Her father had been a count, and her mother an unknown gypsy girl. She had spent time at all the great courts of Europe, and had run away to China when she was twelve. She could speak a dozen languages, and read the moon and the stars. She had been forced to marry a former Russian prince when she was fourteen, but had escaped on a ship to Egypt, where she had trained as a dancer. She could speak to the birds, tame wild horses and divine unknown wells.

No wonder Gobhlachan fell in love with her. Unless, of course, it was the other way round: that she became all these things because of his love. But love it was, and gradually over time Archie was eased out of Gobhlachan's life, as the sun extinguishes the clouds, or as the ocean erodes the land.

This coincided with a rapid decline in Gobhlachan's trade. Once the initial effects of the *Siabadh Mòr* were dealt with – once the pots and pans were repaired, once the barns and houses were rebuilt, once the ploughs and carts were remade – the need for the smithy's services faded away. All that was left were Olga's horses and the needs of the few natives who clung on to the old ways, keeping a horse when a tractor would have been much more useful, using a plough when a combine was much more effective, repairing things when they could now as cheaply be bought brand new.

It seemed overnight – but of course it was years – that things changed. One day, horses were there; the next, none but Olga's existed. One day, people walked to church; the next, they moved in rows on buses. One day, people would tell each other news; the next, they were all sitting in their living rooms, receiving news from places called Beirut and Baghdad.

It was just a different story, of course: the fantastic was now out there, rather than near, happening to strangers on television rather than to themselves in their own villages.

'Did you see that man walking on the moon last night?' they asked each other.

'Did you see that young naked girl going up in flames?'

'Did you see the mushroom cloud, rising and rising and rising?'

Because these picture-stories were told by educated men, most people believed them. After all, there were photographs and films to demonstrate their truth – that girl truly was burning; that former city was shown in all its ashen ruins; that man was heard speaking, as if from underwater, bouncing on the actual surface of the moon.

'Aye, but they'll never land on the sun!' someone said.

Gobhlachan looked at him with pity. 'Of course they will. At night. When it's not so hot.

'These are just the same stories as I told,' he said.

Of course, people laughed at him.

'What? That old fool? Aye, I always knew he was without balls, but that certainly gives a new meaning to be without marbles.'

But every time he saw a new horror, or a new marvel, he knew that it was just a modern version of his own old story, the story of the girl and the bull and the cow and the dragon and the king. He knew all along that kidnappings and rape and conquest and adventure and slaughter and victory were elements of the story, just as the fire and the flames and the bellows and the anvil and the hammer and tongs were the elements out of which he used to make pots and pans and horseshoes and axles and spades and ploughs.

He lived a long time, did Gobhlachan, latterly sitting on his ancient anvil outside the door, like a memorial of himself. The anvil, like the forge, was cold and unused and all the young people would pity him as they drove by, for 'having that bit of cold iron sticking right into his arse'. But Gobhlachan himself was oblivious to the cold, as he watched the young people drive by.

And then one day, something happened. Planes deliberately flew into buildings, and folk began to shake as they watched it all unfolding before their very eyes. Only those who had already lived through The Great Shaking kept a sense of perspective, knowing that they'd seen it all before, somewhere else – where was it now? – in Jerusalem at the time of the Crusades, or at the Somme in the timeless sunshine, or when the young girl was taken away by the white bull and used and abused for years and years and years before she was finally rescued and taken back home to live happily ever afterwards?

Archie was one of those who both shook in his boots and remembered. Unemployed now for years – obviously there was no need of him at a smithy which no one used – and with the tangle market having long gone, conquered by plastics and technology and cheaper markets, he spent his time in that half-world between guilt and hopelessness which is the map of the unemployed.

'Why don't you move off your backside,' his wife would shout at him now and then, 'and get a job like everyone else?' As if jobs were that easy to find in this wilderness. 'That Gobhlachan messed you up is what I say,' she would then mutter, 'with his mad stories and his mad wife. Your problem is that you spent far too much time with that good-for-nothing eunuch when you were younger. Turned you into a useless dreamer instead of a man who can do a damn thing around the house.'

As with all stories, these were fabrications, of course. Hadn't he built the house in the first place, concrete block by concrete block? Hadn't he drained and fenced and ploughed and harrowed and harvested the land for over thirty years? Hadn't he built the boat which lay dry-docked at the end of the house? Hadn't he built the shed and the henhouse and the pigsty and the barn and the outdoor aviary which housed all their livestock, from cockerels to goats? Hadn't he actually married her, against all his better judgment, in a moment of weakness, and fathered that useless son of hers, spoiled by her, who now lounged about every day watching television and trawling the inter-net as if nothing on earth or in heaven mattered except what came out of a screen?

When the smithy unofficially closed down all these years ago, Archie was devastated. By that time he'd been there for ten years – was now twenty-four years of age – and had known little else but the bellowing of the forge and the pouring and the moulding of ore.

Those freezing days cutting the tangle on the shore were an ancient memory and the ten years at the smithy had seemed both an instant and an eternity. Gobhlachan and Olga were, of course, living as man and wife, even though people muttered that they still didn't know which was the man and which the wife. The initial great repairs done, in these years the smithy increasingly turned to the making of domestic furniture and car parts, all of which seemed – to Archie as well as to Gobhlachan and Olga – like the gods turning to croquet, or like making a puddle out of the ocean.

So Archie would spend hours welding a wing onto a car, or polishing the bumper of a lorry, or sawing wood for garden furniture, while his mind was ablaze with the former glory when the hot ore was poured like a waterfall into the mould to emerge, scalded then frozen, as a sword or a ploughshare.

But even the crumbs of the gods mouldered and faded, and within the ten years official garages were set up which undercut and outworked the old smithy. Domestic furniture was the same. Who now wanted a roughly crafted chair or bed or table from Gobhlachan or his man Archie, when a beautiful, smooth chair, at half the price and less, could be bought in the local store, or sent by courier through the post?

Latterly, Gobhlachan and Archie would just sit by the warm forge making nothing but stories which in the end proved more durable than even the iron, which now lies rusting in forgotten fields.

On his last day working with him, Gobhlachan took the burning tongs out of the fire and said to Archie, 'Before you leave me, I have one thing to teach you, which may be even more valuable than the stories. Bring me that board of wood.' And Archie fetched over an ancient board which had lain unused in the corner of the smithy for all these years.

'Watch,' said Gobhlachan, and plunged the burning tongs into the barrel of cold water. He began to make scratches in the wood, burning black marks deep and narrow, curved and rounded, large and small. 'The alphabet,' he said to Archie, proudly, staring at the eighteen Gaelic letters. 'Do you know that out of these eighteen signs you can make the whole world?' he smiled. 'Not quite as good as pictures, but useful. And always remember that you're from a disadvantaged culture – an oral one. After all, they tell me the English have twenty-six of these signs and the Chinese five thousand!' He laughed, putting the tongs back into the fire, where they began again to simmer and glow.

'Did I ever tell you the story about the magic of words?' And while the tongs burned, Gobhlachan said this to Archie:

Once upon a time, there lived a man at Appin in Argyllshire and he took to his house an orphan boy. When the boy was grown up, he was sent to herd; and upon a day of days, and him herding, there came a fine gentleman where he was, who asked the boy to become his servant and said that he would give him plenty to eat and drink, and clothes and great wages.

The boy told him that he would like very much to get a good set of clothes, but that he would not engage till he would see his own master first. But the fine gentleman wanted him engaged without any delay. This the boy would not do, however, upon any terms until he had first seen his own master.

'Well,' says the gentleman, 'in the meantime, write your name in this book.' On saying that, he put his hand into his oxter pocket and, pulling out a large red book, he told the boy to write his name in the book. This the boy would not do. Neither would he tell the gentleman his name till he spoke with his own master first.

'Now,' says the gentleman, 'since you will neither engage, nor tell your name till you see your present master, be sure then to meet me about sunset tomorrow, at a certain place.' The boy promised that he would be sure to meet him at the place about sun-setting.

When the boy came home, he told his master what the fine gentleman had said to him. 'Poor boy,' says he, 'a fine master he would make. Lucky for you that you neither engaged nor wrote your name in his book, but since you promised to meet him, you must go. But as you value your life, do as I tell you.'

His master gave him a sword, and at the same time told him to be sure and be at the specific place mentioned a while before sunset, and to draw a circle round himself with the point of the sword in the name of the Trinity. 'When you do this, draw a cross in the centre of the circle, upon which you will stand yourself. And do not move out of that position till the rising of the sun next morning.'

He also told him that the gentleman would ask him to come out of the circle to put his name in the book, but that upon no account was he to leave the circle. 'But ask for the book, saying that you will write your name in it yourself, and once you get hold of the book, keep it. He cannot touch a hair of your head if you keep inside the circle.

So the boy was at the place long before the gentleman made his appearance, but sure enough he made his appearance after sunset. He tried all his arts to get the boy to step outside the circle, to sign his name in the red book, but the boy would not move one foot out of where he stood. But at long last, he handed the book to the boy so that he would write his name therein himself.

The book was no sooner inside the circle than it fell out of the gentleman's hand. The boy cautiously stretched out his hand for the book, and as soon as he got hold of it, he put it under his oxter. When the fine gentleman saw that the boy did not mean to give him back the book, he grew furious; and he transformed himself into a great many likenesses, blowing fire and brimstone out of his mouth and nostrils. At times he would appear as a horse, other times a huge cat and a fearful beast. He was going round the circle the whole length of the night. When day was beginning to break, he let out one fearful screech; he put himself in the likeness of a large raven and he was soon out of the boy's sight.

The boy still remained where he was till he saw the sun in the morning, which no sooner he observed than he took to his soles home as fast as he could. He gave the book to his master, and that is how the far-famed red book of Appin was got.

Gobhlachan smiled again, taking the red-hot tongs out of the fire. He drew a huge, perfect circle round the eighteen letters of the alphabet, then handed the tongs to Archie, saying, 'And remember, Archie, the circle can be as big, or as small, as you like. As big as the whole world, if you want. As small as a sixpence, if you choose.'

Archie remembered the globe he once saw in the school, which now seemed so small and far away.

2

SO WHEN ARCHIE left to go on his travels to find the source of the north wind, he was pretty much an innocent abroad, yet as wise as the oldest owl in the universe.

He was forty-seven years of age, but had hardly ever been to what was called The Mainland, though that didn't mean that he had cabbage growing behind his ears. He'd been there, of course, a few times: to a football match and a wedding and a funeral and to various offices to sign various forms. And during these forays, he had seen all the usual things which were less than marvellous to him: trains and planes and hovercrafts and violence and snogging and mobile phones.

He'd never stood gobsmacked as a train chug-chug-chugged out of a railway station, or as yet another jumbo jet ascended into the skies, or as yet another pornographic film rolled by on the screen, as it did that time he was in London. He could take it all or leave it. If truth be told, he missed the wind and the rain and the sea and Gobhlachan's stories and John the Goblin's small attempts at extortion every time he set foot in the large cities.

Of course, he would transport his own world with him: the green- and blue-jerseyed football players on the park were really Olga's old grey and dappled horses galloping from one goalpost to the other. The advertising boards flashing messages across the skies were clouds signifying westerly rain: mackerel-shaped haze meant stormy weather; a flashing rainbow signified coming thunder.

Only once, ever, did he see something that really astonished him, and that was when he saw a group of youths kicking an old crippled woman in a doorway, for no reason that he could tell. They didn't even take her handbag or purse, as thieves did in the old stories, before they were executed.

So when Archie decided to go and find the source of the north wind to stop up the hole it came from, his journey was taken neither through ignorance nor through some kind of great existential quest.

He knew full well the very latest meteorological truths, or fictions – he had checked all the dictionaries and the atlases and the search engines, and fully knew that modern scientists claimed that the wind did not just come out of a hole, despite all the evidence to the contrary.

When you built a wall, and left a tiny chink in it, where the hell else did the wind come from except through that tiny hole?

When you bought the latest all-weather, all-singing, all-dancing, thermal, Gore-tex, technology-force jacket with aquafoil pockets and retractable hood system, where still did the wind creep in except through that tiny hole next to your neck which had been pierced by the screwdriver you unfortunately left in the pocket of the attached fleece that last time you washed it, even though the washing instructions clearly stated that it ought not to go anywhere near a washing-machine but ought, instead, to be dry-cleaned and air-dried? But still the hole was there, sending a millizilchmetre of wind right into the hollow of your neck, like a nozzled cold spray straight from the Arctic, or was it the Antarctic? You never quite could remember which.

Nor was his journey Homeric, nor even Joycean. It wasn't some epic journey to the North Pole to stand triumphant with a flag like Roald Amundsen. No – he was merely driven to it by that incessant whistling north wind, which never ceased, even on the stillest of summer days. Even then, as he lay quietly in the middle of a cornfield making music through a grass stalk and admiring the brilliant blue of the sky, he could hear that thin whistle far off, like some kind of insolent boy at the front of the class absently whistling as he rattled off yet another sum to get, once again, twenty out of twenty the smart-ass, while Archie still lumbered at the back of the class counting not just how many fingers he had, but how many toes he didn't have and wished he had. It was blasphemous. Like whistling in church.

But mostly, if truth be told, it was her. Whining like an endless north wind, icily frigid in her talk, cold and dismissive in her comments, moaning and wheezing and complaining and droning in the corner that he was a failure. A layabout, a sluggard, a useless article, a man – if that's what the world called it – unworthy of her love and affection and demands and presence. That's what he really wanted to stop up. Himself. That's what he really wanted to end, and because he did not have the courage to confess it he wandered to the outer limits of the earth to deny it.

Was that what drove Ulysses to the ends of the earth – a nagging wife or mother? What was it that really drove Hillary to the top of Everest, Livingstone to the heart of the earth, Magellan and Drake and Barents and Shackleton to their deaths?

Ulysses himself never really wanted to go off to Troy: he knew that the official reason for the war, the dissemination of the culture of Hellas, was only a pretext for the Greek merchants, who were seeking new markets. When the recruiting officers arrived, Ulysses actually happened to be out ploughing. He pretended to be mad. Thereupon they placed his little two-year-old son in the furrow. Here was the only man in Hellas who was against the war, the father of a young child.

So many stories vindicated Archie. Those stories about the wicked stepmother and the banshees and the *graugaich* and the seal-women and the gorgons and the temptresses. Women, all women, or half-women, who lured men to their fates. The *Bean-Shìth* herself, of course, and the Elle-maid and the Carlin of the Spotted Hill, the Wife of *Ben-y-Ghloc*, the *Glaistig*, the *Gruagach Bàn*… but my goodness, the men, those men with horns and scales and superhuman strength, these inventive scapegoats for real men's sexual and physical and emotional abuse, you never saw or heard or believed anything like it, from the Blue Men of Mull to the Water-Horses of Everywhere, from the Three-Headed Giant to the very Devil himself.

Like all departures, Archie's departure for the North Pole was neither spontaneous nor impulsive. It was long-hatched at the back of the cave, or deep underwater – whichever metaphor you prefer, where Archie abided in that sweet and sour place where all things are born, and die. There, the world was his oyster, or his lobster, as the other man said.

There he understood all the languages of the world and their known and unknown symbols, not just the eighteen that represented his own native language, but the thousands upon thousands that represented all the living and dead and still-to-be-invented languages of the world. There, also, he understood none of them – not even his own indigenous language, small and tiny as it was, with just eighteen simple symbols.

What, after all, did they mean? Nothing. Absolutely nothing, by and in and for themselves, until you mixed them up in the proper order, like the way his mother used to make porridge, first soaking the meal overnight, then cooking it over a slow fire for exactly seven-and-a-half minutes.

That was in those pre-electronic days when the timing was almost genetic, measured by the cockerel's marching backwards and forwards on the spar of the barn. Backwards fifteen times and forwards sixteen times was the proper amount of time needed to bring the porridge meal to the correct consistency, when you then added a dollop of fresh milk – in those days, of course, more like cream than milk – to the top of the porridge, which he called *brochan*, though his immediate neighbours, whose great-great-grandfather had immigrated down from Lewis, still called it by that emigrant name *lit*.

So you mixed the words like that, Archie knew, from the raw material you had though he didn't know how to do it because he'd never really learnt. Oh, he'd gone to school sure enough – he remembered that, but these were different words and symbols that they had presented to him, in which he was not terribly interested at the time, and more's the pity, for they would come in really useful now that he was setting off on this great journey and would surely go through places where he would need to know how to mix these words together to get what he wanted, or to find out where he was going, or to ask what things meant, and could mean, or might mean.

He was as ignorant really, he understood, as the celebrated *gloic* – the fool – in the old stories, who never knew anything about anything, but somehow always triumphed because he ultimately gave the simple, and therefore the right, answer.

Brought before the great king, the *gloic* was asked by the mighty one how much the moon weighed.

He thought for a moment then said, 'One hundredweight!'

'And how do you make that out?' asked the king.

'Well, it comes in four quarters,' said the fool, 'and everyone knows that four quarters make a hundredweight.'

'How many stars are there in the sky, then?' the king asked.

The fool looked up at the starry sky. He imagined the biggest number he could think of, and said 'Seven million, three hundred thousand, eight hundred and forty-five. Exactly.' The king looked at him.

'How do you know?'

'Well,' said the fool, 'I'm fast at counting, and if you think differently, your majesty, just you count them and see how far out I am!'

So finally, the king asked '*A ghloic* – can you tell me where the centre of the earth is?' The gloic looked down at his bare feet.

'Why, right here, just where I'm standing, your majesty. Right here under my feet.'

All that, and so much more, was inside Archie's head, though he was of course very anxious whether any of that stuff would be any good whatsoever to him once he set out on his great adventure, out there into the big wide world. At the bottom of the sea, the boat sank. While everyone sailed, the boat sank. While they were having their tea. An old woman looked up, a scone in her mouth, and seaweed sailed past the window. Fish, as in an aquarium, floated outside the glass. Bodies floated upwards, till he reached the bottom of the sea where he sat, whistling. But no one drowned as they blogged, imagining that they were on board a submarine. No one noticed that the hatches were all open, ready to swallow them.

But you're mature, he would tell himself, bubbling underwater. You've nothing to be afraid of. But he knew enough about dragons and monsters and devils to know otherwise. Were Gobhlachan's wild stories really stories? Were they true somewhere else, as in those olden books he often remembered where maps were drawn with big capital letters marking DANGEROUS SWAMPS HERE and MONSTERS and THE LAIRS OF DRAGONS?

Of course, no monster or dragon would be idiotic enough to stick such huge warning signs up, he was sure of that. In this coalition age, ideology was nameless. No one had the guts to say they really despised the poor.

More likely, if the Bible were true, and he had no reason to doubt it, danger would come unmarked, temptation would come glistening, death would come not in the form of an ugly serpent but – what was it said again? – in the guise of light.

COME IN HERE, it would say in sparkling lights. SEXUAL THRILLS A-PLENTY, the signs in London had said. GOOD GIRLS, CLEAN GIRLS. ASIAN. SOUTH AMERICAN. EAST EUROPEAN. MCDONALD'S – THE FINEST BURGERS IN THE WORLD. ROLEX. CHRYSLER. MARLBORO – THE GENTLEMAN'S CHOICE. CHEQUES CASHED. FREE BANKING. CHANGE THAT WORKS FOR YOU. EIN VOLK, EIN REICH, EIN FÜHRER. THAT'LL DO NICELY.

What a manifesto! The water-horse was always beautiful and sleek until it rushed with you, mane flying and nostrils on fire, beneath the ocean. The gorgeous red-haired woman who lay beside you in bed had her claws in your eyes before sunrise. The cheery small green man who piped you into the knoll, then kept you locked there forever, trapped in an endless dance. Some forbidden joy always led you astray.

He would be careful. Oh aye, he'd be careful all right. No long-thighed lassie would entice him. No musical genius would draw him into his cave. No talons. No mermaids with glistening dresses. No coalitions. No deals. No compromises. No talking birds. Least of all ravens. And he would carry a piece of iron with him. Aye, that would be it. Not a huge bar so as to attract attention to himself. Just a small piece of iron on his person – a locket, or a key, or a nail on a string, or a penknife. A pot stoup from Gobhlachan's old dump would do. Oh, and a circle – he would definitely draw a circle round himself, with a cross at the very centre and never, ever, leave that circle. Let them come and find him, if they could – let them enter the magic circle, if they dare. Let them hand him all their books of magic, and he would hold on to them – those books which gave them wealth and power and influence and beauty and all the rest.

The circle was endless, and he crossed himself amen.

But how to tell her and that son, lying there pressing buttons in front of the television? Well, really, he wouldn't care anyway – he would likely shrug his shoulders, as if he was hearing something from a different channel which he didn't want to watch. And he didn't care, and he really did shrug his shoulders, as if the channel was in a foreign language, which it was.

How to approach her – how to tell her? Would he just blurt out the truth, that he was leaving, going on an expedition – God, how she would sneer and laugh at that word – expedition!

'Expedition!' she would say. 'Who do you now imagine you are? Robert Bloody E. Peary? Doctor Livingstone, I presume?'

And he would be ashamed of himself and say, 'No. Well, really… what I mean is, not so much an expedition as… as…'

As what? A journey? Phwa! A quest? An odyssey? Ha-ha-bloody-ha!

'You're what?' she said, when it came to it and he came in to her all dressed up with a brown suitcase in one hand. She was sitting curled up in the corner seat of the sofa cutting her toenails with a large pair of scissors when he entered with the news. She looked up at him in absolute astonishment – that itself was a joy and a surprise – and almost dropped her scissors.

In the old stories, when the hero left the house the woman would invariably be baking – three kinds of bannocks, a large one and a middling one and a small one.

'Would you like the small bannock with my blessing, the middling bannock with my indifference, or the large bannock with my curse?' the woman would ask and the greedy eldest son, of course, would ask for the large bannock, no matter the consequence, the middle son for the middling bannock and the fair-haired young son (although often he was also the fool) would, of course, ask for the small bannock and the mother's blessing.

But she just sat there laughing at him, half her toenails pared, the other half curled and thick and yellow.

'Would you like me to bring anything back to you?' he heard himself asking, as if he was just popping out to the pub or the village store.

'What about a snowman?' she asked, without a smile. 'You know, one of those ones which are so perfect until they melt.'

God, he thought to himself, she actually has a sense of humour. Why had he never noticed it before? Or had she just discovered it, right at this moment when he was about to leave? Had his decision caused her to melt, as it were? Maybe, he thought, this woman is a completely different woman from the one I thought I knew. Maybe I don't know the first thing about her.

Maybe she was the North Pole. From where the wind blew. The hole from which everything emerged. What if instead of going to find the source of the north wind, he was now actually standing at base camp preparing to walk away from the font? Going in the wrong direction, like a man blinded by the snow, walking in endless circles to his death? Captain Oates going out for some time.

She was now back paring her nails, so he lifted his suitcase and left, determined not to look back, not wanting to be confused by the marks of his own footprints going round and round in the swirling snow behind him.

Many had died that way. Instead of marching on, they had glanced back and mistaken the footprints in the snow for the footprints of someone else, and followed their own prints to an endless death. Or had fallen over precipices, or into ravines or glaciers. Or turned into pillars of salt.

He walked out through the village knowing that they were all standing behind the curtains gazing at him. Archie with his suitcase.

'I wonder where he's going?'

'To the shop?'

'With a suitcase? You must be joking!'

'Away.'

'Yes. Yes, that'll be it. Away.'

'Aye, but away where?'

'Och, the usual! Glasgow. London. Away. Far away.'

'And no wonder! How long would you have stayed with her?'

'Or with him!'

'Poor Bella! She'll be thankful for it. Aye, she'll be fine.'

And the bus disappeared north, Archie making a circle in the steamed window. His nose pressed to the glass, watching the fields and the rocks bump by. A brown cow stared at the bus. A seagull sat on a fence-post. Someone went by on a bicycle. A child sat cuddling a pet lamb outside a porch. The school travelled by, the church sat impassive on the high hill.

Through the villages the bus travelled. John and Donald and Wilma and Joina came on the bus and all came off at the hospital. Four young people with backpacks came on the bus at the pier and spoke to each other in a foreign language two seats behind Archie. He recognised the occasional English word – 'iPod' and 'Michael Schumacher', but the rest was indistinguishable.

Maybe 'Michael Schumacher' is not an English word – or words – he thought. German. Though Michael Schumacher was probably Michael Schumacher in any language. Even in Gaelic, Archie thought, though he would pronounce it *Mìcheal Schumacher*.

On the ferry, he recognised and nodded to various people he knew. He didn't need to talk to them because they were all speaking to someone else on their mobile phones. He checked his own, which only had a Vodaphone message. Free weekend calls. Handy. He drank a pint of beer and ate fish and chips in the ferry cafe, and was soon on the mainland bus travelling south through Skye.

Strange. Going south to go north, he thought. The Cuillin shrouded in mist to his right. South, south. North. East. South. West. The school compass. North, nor-nor-east, nor-east, east-nor-east, east, east-sou-east, sou-east, sou-

sou-east-east, south, sou-sou-west, sou-west, west-sou-west, west, west-nor-west, nor-west, nor-nor-west, north. I could have gone directly north. To Lewis. And then? There wasn't a ferry from Stornoway to the Arctic, was there?

The Cal-Mac office: 'A ticket to the Arctic, please.'

He could see that girl in the office – what was her name again – Joan? – with that cynical tongue of hers. 'And would that be a Single, Archie, or a five-day Open Return?'

He could go via Shetland, of course. The bus to Inverness, train to Thurso or Aberdeen, and the boat to Lerwick, like the fisher girls – *clann-nighean an sgadain.* Another boat from there to the Faeroes, and Bob's your uncle. A single step from there to the Circle. There was a Pole Hill in Sutherland, and a Polperro in Cornwall. Maybe even Polynesia came from the Gaelic word Poll, meaning mud.

But when he woke he was in Fort William. Just as well continue. I'll get a plane from Glasgow to Sweden, or somewhere up there, he thought, see who's cheapest.

Glencoe. Where the black Campbells murdered the innocent Macdonalds. Ben Dòrain sweeping by all bare to the left, without honour. And money! Good as the credit cards in his wallet looked, the bank balance itself was pretty dodgy. Especially since it was a joint account and good old Bellag would instantly have got a taxi out to the well and drained a few bucketfuls from it. Damn it. What the hell. Surely Fionn MacCool never bothered much about his bank account. Just what he had. His hound and his skill.

And he slept again, dreaming about anvils and flames and the whirling of the forge: the sound of the bus engine idling down at Buchanan Street Station. Everest base-camp. He walked down Sauchiehall Street, whistling for strength.

3

ARCHIE SPENT HIS first night in Glasgow in a fine hotel.

He counted his money, and discovered that – really – he had plenty. This was not going to be a poverty-stricken, penny-pinching expedition, surviving on dead rats and old bits of hardened broken biscuits. Such deprivation had broken the spirits of greater men: Savonarola going mad for lack of air, Galileo dying for sight of the sun, Captain Scott for a deficiency of fruit.

This he knew: for want of a nail the world was lost. Archie fingered the nail he'd brought with him from the old forge, just in case.

On the other hand, he didn't want to go to the other extreme either. Excessive luxury was just as deadly. Genghis Khan growing fat and corpulent on cheese and wine. Alexander the Great overdosing on women. Or was it men? He couldn't quite remember. Not that it made much difference in the end.

In the inter-net zone in the lobby of the hotel Archie sat at his booth and Googled in the simple things. 'Where does the wind come from?' 'What is the North Pole?' 'What is north of the North Pole?' He sat studying the answers, which were almost as remarkable as Gobhlachan's eternal puzzles.

There was the Geographic North Pole, of course. But also, apparently, the Magnetic North Pole and the Geomagnetic North Pole and the Northern Pole of Inaccessibility. But the only thing that remained with Archie was this: 'Geographic North defines latitude 90 per cent. In whichever direction you are travelling from here, you are always heading south.'

'That's it!' said Archie. To go forever south, even if it was west or east or north or south. But then again, he realised, these notions would be completely meaningless at the Pole itself. There would be no north or east or west – just south. Maybe that was the case everywhere. Perhaps there was no north or west or east or south anywhere. They were just ways of putting things, like the ways in which Gobhlachan would put things in a story, or in the smithy. Where this thing larger than yourself was called a giant, and this other thing smaller than yourself was called a dwarf, and this thing that took you away was called a bull or a horse or a fairy or a toad. And the thing that was dangerous was called an enemy, though sometimes too he was called a friend.

And if that was true of the Pole, must it not also be true of the wind? This thing that swept across the globe and had killed so many that day, taking every roof and outhouse, every cart and plough, every living being with it in its outstretched arms? Which then stroked your face on a summer's day. Did it really have sinewy muscles and full-blown-out-cheeks as in the old illustrations, or was that just a way of putting things? Did it actually start somewhere – was there an oven, or a forge, or a smithy, or a hole, or a machine out of which it came, like a baby, or a foal, or a calf or a potato, which, after all, grew and grew and grew from a small seed? The great story of God and the seed of the wind.

He looked about him in the airless lobby, men all crouched over their laptops or terminals. A singular woman sat in the corner fanning herself with a newspaper. Flies buzzed about the rows of strip-lights above the computer booths. Through the thick double-glazed windows vehicles moved soundlessly outside. There must have been a wind, for suddenly a discarded chip-box flew through the air and a garage door opposite began to open and close haphazardly.

How it would come in the early spring, sprinkling the ground with blossom and flowers. And how it would serve as a magic carpet for the bees in May-time, moving them from one purple clover to the other. And how – during those hot days when he bent over the peat in the heather – the warm wind would come and relieve him instantly of the flies and midges and clegs which lay in their thousands all over his bitten body. And then there were those autumn days when he used to go fishing, and he had to literally push the boat out into the water because it was so still and calm and how he had to row out for miles beyond the Lighthouse Point (*Rubh' an t-Solais*) before he could catch the wind which was trapped behind the high ridge, but once you hit the Point there it came, that old friend, softly touching your face and riffling his fingers through your hair and raising the collar of your cotton shirt before he punched the sails which all of a sudden filled with his spirit and flew, like a kite, across the water as you flung out the net behind, in the vain hope of catching the silver darlings.

And one night – oh, this was a long time before Bella – how he had lain with Christina in the barley sheaves, with the wind flinging the awns about their heads and the grain in their eyes and ears and hair as they lay twined in the stubble which neither of them noticed or felt till afterwards, when they lay back awkwardly staring up at the breeze moving the golden spikelets between them and the sky.

That was the day of the wren: the day the wren came and

rested on Christina's hand as she lay sleeping, with not a breath of air stirring in the whole universe.

So Archie typed in 'wind'. Or, more precisely: 'Where does the wind come from?'

And this marvel before him displayed an answer which convinced him.

'It all starts with the sun,' says Professor Kimberley Strong, an expert in atmospheric physics at the University of Toronto. Solar radiation emitted by the sun travels through space and strikes the Earth, causing regions of unequal heating over land masses and oceans. This unequal heating produces regions of high and low pressure.

The atmosphere tries to equalise those pressures, so you get movement of air from a region of high pressure to a region of low pressure. Scientists call this the pressure of gradient force, and it is the fundamental force behind wind.

Earth's rotation adds a twist to the story. While wind would normally move in a straight line, the spinning of the planet beneath makes the wind appear to follow a curved path. This is known as the Coriolis effect, which deflects winds to the right in the northern hemisphere and to the left in the southern hemisphere. There is no Coriolis effect at the equator. The faster the wind blows, the more it is deflected by the spinning of the Earth.

'Ah,' thought Archie, 'it all starts with the sun! So I need to go to the sun.' But he knew the things that were impossible. He would burn. Even at night-time. In the old Gaelic story the wind and the sun had a contest.

A small boy is going to school on a cold winter's day, with his coat wrapped tightly around him.

'Of course I'm stronger that you,' boasted the wind, swirling around the weak sun. And there, hidden behind the dark clouds, the sun brooded, like Gordon Brown; quiet, fully aware of her own strength and power.

'I'll show you,' roared the wind. 'Do you see that small boy down there? That insect-like creature crawling along the ground down there on the earth? I bet I can force his coat off before you can!' And the wind filled up his lungs and puffed out his cheeks and blew and raged and roared and the more he blew the tighter the wee boy fastened his coat round his body, turning his back to the angry, exhausted wind.

'Ah!' said the sun, stretching herself out beyond the clouds, her million slender fingers pushing all the darkness to one side, 'Now let me glow.'

And she shone, bright and red and hot. And the small boy, steam rising from his soaking coat, began to perspire, finally flinging off his coat and lying down on the drying grass, staring up into the electric blue sky, a grass stalk idly stuck between his whistling lips.

And the wind sulked, off back into his cave, to regather for another day.

Archie left the hotel and walked down Sauchiehall Street in the evening light. Incredible how short the girls' skirts all were. He stood a while in the doorway of a store called Topshop looking at folk streaming by, much like tides on the shoreline. He caught sight of himself in the shop mirror, the beard stubble rooting white, the hair thinning. How had he grown so old all of a sudden? In a single night. He remembered John the Goblin, who would have been well over eighty now, had he survived. Cancer, after all these roll-ups. Though he was still leaping across the sand dunes in the mirror, his fag tin shimmering in the sun in the back pocket of his trousers.

Was he John Goblin to those rushing by? If he existed. Where did the old go on a Friday evening, anyway? Did they abandon the town centres – were they bussed out to the bingo-halls in the suburbs – or had they been shipped out there anyhow a long time ago, never to return? How they had all gone to Canada, sailing like handkerchiefs.

He went into a pub, but it was like nothing he remembered. No smoke. Poor John Goblin. No one playing dominoes or pool or cards: just huge throbbing music and vast video screens perched above every corner of the room, where even more young women with bare navels gyrated across the heavens. These were no giants, but giantesses, lithe and lissome and willowy. On some of the screens men played football, as seen from above: they moved like pawns, or warriors, across the starry sky.

Archie asked for a beer and was given a bottle, without a glass. He looked around him and saw that all the young people in the bar were drinking just like that, right out of the bottle. He felt at home. That's what he'd always done, swilling down a whole bottle of milk in the heather, or a whole bottle of ale at the machair, or a whole half-bottle of whisky at the fank. This was just home with different pictures and music.

He smiled at two young women standing at the bar next to him. They smiled back. 'Noisy,' he tried to say to them, but the music drowned out the word and by the time he thought of another word they'd gone, carrying their drinks on a tray into the darkness.

A man was standing on the other side, so he tried the same word on him, but he just put his hand to his ear and shook his head, meaning: 'Listen, mate, there's absolutely no point in trying to talk in here. We're like fish underwater, gawping at each other. Words can't be heard here, so don't even bother trying.' And he too had gone, carrying his single beer bottle in his hand to the middle of the floor, where a crowd was dancing in sacred circles of their own, gesticulating to one another.

Don't do it, a voice inside Archie's head said. Whatever you do, don't make an idiot of yourself by going out there and dancing. And since it was the only voice which he could hear, Archie listened. But then the surprising thing happened – this girl came up to him and handed him a piece of paper on which was written: 'Hi. My name is Jewel. Would you like to dance?'

'Yes. Yes, of course I would,' he said as she took him by the hand and led him to the centre of the crowded floor, where all the young people moved backwards and forwards, each with an open bottle in hand.

Jewel swayed to and fro in front of him like – well, like a jewel, of course, all glittering and shining in a silver top with sparkling purple trousers; though Archie thought of her more as a spray of the ocean, the way in which on a late spring day when the tide changes, the sea itself rises higher and moves in, splashing senselessly against the rocks.

Holding on to his bottle, he managed to keep sight of Jewel as she moved round the floor, occasionally making rapid hand signals to friends she passed as she danced, occasionally pecking other girls on the cheek, occasionally greeting other dancers with a sharp clapping noise of her palms, going rat-a-tat-tat, tat-a-tat-tat. It took Archie the whole beat of the dance and more to realise that all these young people were actually talking to each other in sign language.

Just like himself and Gobhlachan. The world interpreted through signs. A universe understood with a movement, and misunderstood through some invisible gesture. Archie tried to understand the conversation, but couldn't. The girls would raise a finger, touch an ear lobe, smack the back of a hand with two fingers from the other, while the men pounded a fist against an open palm or brushed a wrist with one, two, three fingers. Archie had no idea where a word or sentence began or ended, or how you distinguished between movement and speech, or when the dance finished and the talk started, as if such mattered. It was all talk or dance.

Jewel suddenly stopped dancing and moved over to a table in the corner, beckoning him to follow.

Once seated, she made a whole series of quick movements with her hands, but halfway through she also clearly understood that he was a foreigner and that he wasn't understanding a single thing she was saying. So she lowered the small pencil from behind her ear and wrote on the stacked pieces of paper set on every table.

'Where are you from?' she wrote.

'Elitrobe,' he wrote back.

'Eh?' she replied.

'What is this?' he asked.

'A club,' she wrote. 'Deaf. But not dumb! Ha!'

'What's your name?' her mouth asked.

'Archie,' he said.

'Look,' she said. She placed the forefinger of her right hand onto the forefinger of her left. 'E,' her mouth said, soundlessly. The same finger to the thumb of the left hand. 'A,' she said. The same finger to the middle finger of the left hand, and he understood that to be 'I'.

How eloquent, the forefinger.

She was from Ayr, though her grandmother was from Lochinver. And he? Travelling. Where? O – north. North? Aye, north. North like Inverness? No. North like Spitsbergen. North like Alaska. North like Nansen. Fridtjof Nansen.

'That far?' her fingers said.

They stopped talking and resumed dancing. For a while, Gobhlachan disappeared.

'Do you believe there's a new story?' he asked her as they danced, though she didn't hear.

But that didn't make much difference. How beautiful she was: tall and slim, like a pole. To carry a creel, the women wore an old *còta*, a loose kilted skirt, rolled up to form a *dronnag*, a creel pad on the lower part of the back, where the creel could rest. Along with a well-made breastband, this made it much easier for women to carry their burdens, and even made it possible for them to carry much heavier loads. The male islander of this period had no desire for women who were tall and slender. Strong, sturdy, broad-backed women who could also help to push the boats up the beaches were appreciated.

Her nails painted red, her body moving endlessly in front of him like the seismographic waves he once saw on an X-ray machine at the local cottage hospital.

Everyone at the club was going to a party at the flat of a couple who'd just gotten engaged that evening – Belfast Tommy and Frieda from Orkney. They had a flat in Ingram Street in the merchant city.

'Come if you want,' she said.

They all walked home together down Hope Street.

McDonald's was still open and some of them went in there. Archie and Jewel entered with them. How bright the lights were after the darkness of the pub. They bought chips and Coke and went upstairs.

'Jewel?' he asked.

'Shorthand,' she wrote back, 'for Julie Ann.'

'Ah!' he said. And added, '*Sìleas* – the Gaelic for Julie. And Jewel means *Seud*.'

'Sìleas Seud then,' she said.

The conversation was broken and fragile, like all conversations. She taught him a little by hand; he wrote now and then. How the club met monthly, on the last Friday. His age. She? Don't ask. Why the invitation-note? Just that she saw him and that he'd reminded her of someone. Her grandfather? At least a laugh. You can recognise danger, other senses compensate for the loss of some. Like the antelopes: they can smell danger beneath the savannah swamp.

'I've got a fortnight,' her fingers said. 'Holidays. Camping in Poolewe, but the Pole will do.'

Another laugh.

'One tent.'

'Two sleeping-bags.'

'Right.'

'Sure, sure.'

'Bird and bush.'

'Fine.'

'Done.'

Since the world was 24/7, a travel agency was still open next to McDonald's, Central Station. It was called GO4U.

'Let's,' their bodies said. 'Let's look anyway.'

And while the others walked down towards Ingram Street, Archie and Sìleas entered the shop, laughing.

Not only was there the usual row of computers where

you could choose your own holiday, but the agency also had a row of desks where the agents sat. They went over to an Indian girl sitting at Desk 5, which was headed Aurora Borealis.

Had they brochures for travelling north? Near the Arctic Circle?

She opened a drawer and handed them four thick brochures – *North Pole Ski Expeditions*; *North Pole Dogsled Expeditions*; *North Pole Champagne Flights*, and one simply called *Seasonal Specials*.

'These are the only brochures we have in stock,' she said. 'They're all run by the one company – the Northwest Passage Polar Adventures Company – though there are others. They of course have a website too, if you want to check that out.' And she wrote *polarexplorers.com*, in a spindly line.

They took the brochures and made their way to Thomas and Frieda's flat. No one bothered much with them. Some danced; some ate; some watched a silent Russian film on DVD; couples hid in various nooks and crannies. The flat had a miniature roof garden and Archie and Jewel climbed up there via the attic stair. They looked at Glasgow, all lit down below them. The silent decorative cranes in Govan, the windmills beyond Bearsden.

They opened one of the brochures.

Day 1 – Meet at Longyearbyen Airport, Norway. Transfer from airport to Lodge. Unpack gear and relax. Opportunity to explore Longyearbyen. Welcome reception and dinner.

Day 2 – Final equipment review, warm-up ski/dogsledding near Longyearbyen. Last chance to get goodies and/or clothing or equipment in town!

Day 3 – Fly to 89 degrees North latitude. Depending on weather conditions, we may immediately depart for 88 degrees north (by helicopter) or we may set up camp and spend the night.

Day 4 through 14 – From 88 degrees, we'll dogsled and ski the final 2 degrees to the North Pole! Days are spent mushing the dogs.

'The last thing on earth I want to do,' said Jewel, 'mushing the dogs, whatever that means.'

Good God, thought Archie, how sweet she smells.

...and skiing. Generally, one or two people work with each dog team while other participants ski.

Jewel: 'But I can't ski!'

Evenings are spent setting up camp, feeding and caring for the dogs...

'And I really hate dogs!' she said.

Day 15 – Arrive at the Geographic North Pole! Enjoy a Polar celebration with champagne...

And I don't drink! thought Jewel.

This itinerary is highly dependent on a number of factors and is subject to change. Price: 22,500 euros.

'I haven't got 22,500 euros,' Archie wrote on a slip of paper, 'and I also hate dogs.'

Jewel opened the fourth brochure.

Seasonal Specials, Santa Holidays, it said.

'Look,' said Jewel, 'that's cheaper. £249 for a round day-trip from Glasgow!'

He was amazed how quickly he was learning to lip-read. He read with her:

At last the elves have revealed the location of the original Post Office of Santa Claus which can be found in a forested setting to the north of Rovaniemi above the Arctic Circle.

How beautiful her fingers were, moving so faithfully across the words.

This day visit will evoke memories of brass counters, sealing wax and Santa's original star navigation system for letter deliveries.

The night was clear and even through the orange streetlights they could see the stars far to the north.

Here in the original Post Office, Santa continues to handle letters from all over the world with the assistance of his elves and looks forward to welcoming you on this auspicious occasion.

What was permitted?

Your day begins with a flight from your local airport to Rovaniemi. Breakfast will be served during your outward flight and where possible aircraft equipped with video entertainment systems will be used.

He remembered another way of travelling. By bonnet. The shepherd who lived by himself in Kintail, in a small bothy, at the back of the ben.

One evening, having lit a fine, the shepherd lay down in the heather-bed he'd made up in the corner. So cold outside, all the animals began to creep in. Twenty cats entered and sat round the fire holding up their paws and warming themselves. One went to the window, put a black cap on its head, cried 'Hurrah for London!', and vanished.

The other cats, one by one, did the same. But when the last cat put the cap on his head, it fell off and the shepherd grabbed the bonnet, stuck it on to his own head and shouted 'Hurrah for London!' And he too disappeared.

He reached London in a twinkling, and with his companions went to drink wine in a cellar. He got drunk and fell asleep. In the morning he was caught, taken before a judge, and sentenced to be hanged. At the gallows he entreated to be allowed to wear the cap he had on in the cellar: it was a present from his mother, and he would like to die with it on. When it came, the rope was already round his neck. He clapped the cap on to his head, and cried 'Hurrah for Kintail!'

He disappeared with the gallows about his neck, and his friends in Kintail, having by this time missed him and being assembled in the bothy prior to searching the hills, were much surprised by his strange appearance.

Wasting nothing, they set to work dismantling the wooden gallows round his neck and turned it into the stern and keel of a boat, which may still be seen fishing in the area in the half-light between sunset and darkness.

It was all there: darkness, loneliness, witchcraft, fleeing, drunkenness, judgement, salvation, humour. He knew it was all before him. Even with a cap, he would not get her, except as a skiff in the memory in the twilight. Jewel's finger said,

> *Following arrival at Rovaniemi Airport, transportation will be provided to Santa's secret location. To protect all members of the group from the cold, appropriate arctic clothing consisting of an all-in-one-suit and boots has been organised. The elves have previously advised us that during December Santa may be seen regularly, close to his post office, supervising the handling of all his present requests, and that he will always spare time to meet with visitors to his Arctic homeland.*

Jewel looked up from the text, her face glowing. She was almost translucent: like one of these gossamer days back home in Gobhlachan's forge when a sudden gust of wind would catch the liquid iron coming out of the kiln and sent fragments of flames up into the sky. You could see through the fragments as they flew, and the remarkable thing was the way in which they transformed the colour of the air. The world altered. That which was dark or red or blue was suddenly luminous and green and yellow. Things invisible became evident.

'Would you teach me?' he wrote on a slip of paper.

'Teach what?' she wrote back.

He splayed his stubby fingers out in a fan-shape in front of his face, holding back the tears. Those thick working fingers which had frozen so long ago in the seaweed. Which had never really done anything gentle or sweet or completely selfless. He wanted to cry out, 'To teach me how to love!' but the words remained frozen inside him. He knew fine he was the deaf-mute, not this limpid, articulate woman sitting before him.

'Damn it,' he said, 'I'll do it!' And taking the sheet of

paper she offered him from her handbag, he wrote, 'Teach me how to be. How to speak. How to feel. How to love. How to hold you.'

She stretched her hand across the table, wiping the solitary tear away from his cheek, and took hold of his hands.

'A,' she mouthed, raising the thumb on his right hand off the table. 'B,' she said, raising the forefinger on the right hand, and in a much gentler way than Gobhlachan, taught him the complete alphabet she knew, from beginning to end.

Not instantly, but over the course of the days and the years, so that he learned how to speak out of the silence, how to communicate with more than mere words. Not just how to hear, as with Gobhlachan, but how to tell. And not just how to tell, but how to conceive and invent.

A universe gathered in her fingertips. And when she touched his forehead or arms or face with her fingers, how electrified he became, and how she removed gravity from him, like a magnet shifting iron. Electromagnetism. The Hadron Collider of Love, as St Paul once put it.

But still there was no union. Despite – or perhaps because of – the quarks and protons, they divided. Despite every fastening, every tactile signal, the gap was too wide. The sea-channel was too broad, and they couldn't quite work our why, except that it was so. Rocks in the way, seaweed clinging to the propeller, the oars uncoordinated. No known bearings, the compass outdated and unreliable, the tiller awry, the lanyard torn. The galleys that had sunk in the Sound of Barra! The burning Viking longships which had foundered on the reefs. She was too young, maybe, or too beautiful, or too perilous. He was too old, perhaps, or too demanding or fearful or fixed. Bearing too many burdens, too much history. Too familiar with the old story to learn a new one. Too rigid for a new fiction, a different gospel.

And that wind began again, small and thin and narrow and far away at first, but so well known to the ear. Maybe that was the problem: the permanent anxiety which fed every movement. A hint of a breeze. A gasp of oxygen. Where doubt enters, certainty departs.

And they separated, like summer from autumn: before you notice, you are in another season.

4

HE REMEMBERED THAT the streets of London were paved with gold, and so took the night bus to the big city through the dark shires of England.

When he woke, it was raining on the motorway. His watch read 05.23 and a sign rushed by saying J63 Service Station. He put his face flat to the darkened window, but could see nothing except more sweeping lights and rain.

He used to sweep the sand dunes with a torch, hunting for rabbits. In those long-ago, pre-television days when all was wind and rain and hope. It took skill. To stalk the hollows by moonlight, the unlit torch gripped in the palm of the hand, listening for the eternal scratching. 'There it is! There!' And with one flick of the switch the whole machair was illuminated.

And caught in the full torch-beam, how the rabbit froze, his eyes bulging with terror before the club fell on his skull. Those glorious pre-myxomatosis days when Archie and all of nature were one.

At Waterloo he checked into a bunkhouse and immediately made his way to the Job Centre. There were loads of jobs for chefs and receptionists and telesales, but finally he spotted something that suited his skills: labourers required for an extension to Terminal 5 at Heathrow Airport. Whatever else he could do, he knew he could push a barrow and wield a spade and mix cement with the best of them.

By the following morning, Archie was where hundreds of thousands of Scots and Irish and Jamaicans had been before: head down a hole, making concrete. You can say what you want about modern technology, and state-of-the-art machinery, and computers-which-design-and-build, but this development still depended upon the thousands of Archies carrying hods of bricks up ladders, screwing scaffolding together, hammering wooden sarking into the ground, sweeping up the rubbish, painting walls, erecting makeshift toilets, nailing notices to the floor, digging holes, filling them up, draining sewage away, clawing underground like wolves, swearing, drinking, betting, cursing. The pay was good.

'Not as good as them fuckin' bastards up there,' the squad would shout, as they watched another jumbo jet set off into space high overhead.

'Think they would fuckin' give us better fuckin' earplugs to fuckin' protect our fuckin' ears, for fuck's sake,' he would hear through the bad ear-muffs the company gave to the workers.

'Daft and deaf, that's us,' someone else would shout. And then, the invariable song:

We're the fucking navvies
Treated like the scavvies,
Building fucking lavvies
For the Ruling Class.

'Away with you, you bastard – we are the Ruling Class,' someone else would shout, before the next mob began their own indecent song:

Heigh-ho, heigh-ho,
We are the working boys!
Heigh-ho, heigh-ho,
Playing with our toys!
We push them and we pull them,
Stick them right inside!
We're talking 'bout our trowels,
Hanging by our side!
Heigh-ho, heigh-ho
We are the working boys!

And they would laugh, rather than cry.

Archie realised that this was a new, brutal vocabulary he had to learn, just as he'd learned Jewel's beautiful sign language and Gobhlachan's fictions. A crushed, broken language, as if everything in the world was reduced to the size of a ball which you hit against... well, take your pick. Themselves. Women.

He'd heard this language before, of course – he wasn't quite that stupid or innocent. But that was from a distance – in the pub, certainly; those other times he'd been in the big city, certainly, and also through television, but he'd never really lived at the centre of it, in this close proximity where it was the rule rather than the obscene exception. And he joined in, of course. Not just because Archie, when in Rome, does what Angelo does, but because it was impossible not to. As with sign language with Jewel, effing this and effing that and effing the other was the only way he could communicate: otherwise when he spoke there were just huge voids in his sentences.

What depressed him was the sheer constant intensity of this language. Working from eight in the morning till six at night gave no respite, no distance, no separation, except for complete silence, for which he would be ridiculed and mocked and shunned. 'You stuck-up, conceited bastard. Who do you think you are? Lord fucking Haw-Haw?' So he just joined in, effing and blinding with all the rest of them as if all language was a stone. Smash smash smash. Whack whack whack. Hah hah fucking hah. Thump thump thump. F f f f. F f f f.

After a week he'd had enough and left, despite the daily dreams that one morning one of those wealthy women he could see high up in the skies in the VIP Lounge which sat high above the building site would break open the triple-glazed glass and shout down, 'Hey, you – Archie! Yes – you with the rippling muscles down there, come here and accompany me to Hawaii. I'm going there for six months and I need a man just like you to drive me to the beach daily!' Despite that myth he could bear it no longer, and left.

So instead of the building site, he found work in that other great refuge of London: in one of the kitchens of a fancy restaurant fronting on to Soho Square. Here all language was really immaterial, for it was full of all kinds of workers from all parts of the globe who couldn't verbally understand each other. What a relief to be in this immigrant heaven of illegal workers, skating around the kitchen in the noise of a thousand languages. What matter if all the words were still fuck, which sounded so variable in all these other languages. In actual fact, the word was hardly uttered, except by the loud-mouthed (and better paid) chefs. They ruled the roost like cockerels in a barn, strutting backwards and forwards demanding this, that and the next.

'Wash that fucking pan, properly! Mix these fucking eggs right! Wipe that pot clean, you bastard! Clear out of my fucking way!'

But their excursions into the kitchen were swift and momentary, and for the most part Archie and his accompanying army of Chinese, Koreans, Latvians, Poles, Nigerians, Kenyans, Moroccans, and God – or Allah – only knows who else, were left to rush around in the Babel of their own languages, washing dishes, scouring pans, wiping floors, peeling potatoes, skinning fish, mashing fruit and a thousand and one other tasks which all served to present a beautiful dinner to these who came though the front door to pay their wages.

And what a crowd they were! The rumour would sweep like a wind though the kitchens: Angelina Jolie is in tonight! Michael Douglas and Zeta! Prince William! Tom Cruise! Sean Connery! Victoria Beckham herself! 'Not arff,' they all shouted, and almost stamped on each other to peek at her through the peephole into the restaurant, to discover whether her tits really were as small as they looked in all these magazines.

On their night off, this international kitchen-staff would all meet down the pub, which is where Archie learned that China and Nigeria and all the rest of these nations also had a Gobhlachan who sat astride a cold anvil, or under a withered eucalyptus tree, or behind a bamboo wall, telling tall tales. The sky was made out of rice in China, while in Malaysia the pores of the apple trees were where Knowledge lived, ready to be scattered or sown all over the world. Ododgubu told him that back in his native village in Kenya the Battle of the Birds (*Cath nan Eun*) had taken place: the tikitikikoota, the lightest bird in the universe, had won by harnessing a lift on the tip of the great Breasted-Eagle's wing. 'He was furthest away from Grugrasinda, the spirit of the mud.'

Arsenal – Arse'n'All, they all pronounced it – was the local football team which they all cheered whenever it appeared on the small television in the pub. Unlike the Glasgow bar, this place in Soho had remained curiously old-fashioned, without music or video screens, so the clientele imagined they were local and treasured. Few of the kitchen staff knew anything about football and cared even less, but nevertheless fell into the pattern of cheering those distant, wealthy heroes whenever they appeared in their red warrior uniforms on the screen.

As it happened, the kitchen uniform was also red: red overalls for both the men and women, which made them all sweat like pigs but made them appear like bright angels in the background to diners who caught a glimpse of them washing and scouring through the eternally swinging kitchen-doors.

Archie became friendly with a Romanian potato-peeler called Sergio and an Irish woman called Angelina, originally from Derry, who specialised in gutting the fish which came fresh every few hours from the Billingsgate market.

'Fresh!' she would guffaw. 'I've seen fresher socks on a tramp after five days!' And she would explain how the fish had come thousands of miles from the Baltic and the Falklands, frozen – 'maybe even several times' – on the way. 'How we haven't killed half the diners already is beyond me. But then again, they're probably impervious to poison by now. As they used to say in the Republic: the rich don't choke on gold!'

Her raw humour was – of course – a cover for her grief. Her parents and two sisters and brothers had been taken in the Omagh bombing when she was ten.

'I happened to have gone inside to the toilet and I heard the bomb go off as I sat there, but by the time I managed to pull my pants up and get back outside they were all dead, scattered in bits all over the street.'

She smoked endlessly, despite the smoking ban, out through the kitchen window, claiming that though her body was inside, all the nicotine was outside.

'After all, I don't smoke through my arse.'

'The smoke was almost the worst thing that day,' she told Archie. 'All klaxons and sirens and police in uniforms.

'Relatives took me, but I never took to them. Then sent me to the nuns, though you'd have thought they'd have known better. Ran away when I was fourteen, joined the Kilkenny circus. Well, when I say the Kilkenny circus I don't mean, of course, that it was a circus from Kilkenny, oh no. Just a small shitty show that was passing through that small shitty town. Not even an elephant. Three small horses they'd picked up in Connemara and a man who juggled his balls all the time. Called himself Marvin the Magnificent. His real name was Bert Slater. He was from Sunderland, which seemed magnificent enough to me. And two Spanish transvestites, Alquino and Alberto, who masqueraded as Alphonse and Ariadne, the king and queen of Spanish acrobatics. God, you should have seen Alberto stuffing cotton wool inside his purple leotard and crushing his balls into a leather pouch strapped tight between his legs. But he did look magnificent, twirling and glittering on that high-bar like the Queen of Sheba, all snaky and sexy. Remarkable what razzle-dazzle can do to your brain.'

Archie knew fine she was talking about him as much as about everything and everyone around her. Like Gobhlachan, for her, the more colourful the story was, the better.

Wasn't there any kind of bare story, which revealed rather than hid the truth? Fact, not fiction. Standing, not running. Staying not moving. But who was he to judge anyone else's tale? Didn't it belong to her, and to her alone? Especially in the telling.

'The Troubles!' she would spit out. 'Now there's a show for you, to be sure. Appearing tonight at your village, no names, no pack drill – The Troubles! Starring Merlin the Magician, who can make thousands disappear at the drop of a bomb! Johnny the Jolly Juggler, who can spin all the Six Counties and make them appear like thirty-eight! Philomena the Fabulous, who can change Terrorists into Freedom Fighters. And of course the Ringmaster himself, who pretends to be in charge. Oh, and don't forget the Clown, who can make us all laugh.'

She often cried at that point. Real tears that came unwanted, without performance, without any whip cracked. She didn't have to say that she was the clown, covering herself with paint and flour and water, walking about with her courageous bravado, in her over-large shoes, her dotted costume, with her bucket and sponge.

On and off, Sergio was her boyfriend, though neither of them ever revealed how they came to be an item, as the saying has it. Maybe it really was as simple as it looked: as if these two young people had bumped into each other in this kitchen, had talked to each other, and became lovers.

Sergio the potato-peeler was a unique breed in the kitchen. While everyone else, Archie and Angelina included, had to be Jacks and Jills of all trades (obviously the restaurant manager, in his weekly briefing, called it 'multi-skilling') Sergio was given an exemption. Some said – and this was just a complete pack of lies – that he was given preferential treatment because Luigi (the restaurant manager) fancied him. Others said that he was given the sole job of potato-peeling simply because he was too dull and stupid to do anything else, though still others argued that it was the very opposite, and that no one else in the whole wide world could peel potatoes so sharply, so swiftly, so accurately and so beautifully for so long.

Which certainly looked like the truth, for to watch him for even a few seconds, potato in one hand and screw-knife in the other, was an utter joy. Like watching Einstein himself in that old newsreel, scrawling that stuff, $E=MC^2$, so very rapidly in chalk on to the old blackboard. One moment the potato would be there, all lumpy and dirty-skinned, and the next, with what appeared to be a single flick of his right wrist, the peel was cascading off in exquisite loops and circles, like a ballerina's leg when she does that swift rolling movement, the *rond de jambe,* which spins against gravity.

'Hey, they should put him out front of house,' all the kitchen staff bellowed. 'What a joy that would be for the diners! An added attraction! A free extra! A bonus! An individual stamp of triumph for this restaurant! Value added!'

Luigi was reluctant at first, but they persisted: 'Don't these foreign restaurants have fish tanks next to the dining tables for you to choose which fish you'll have for your dinner? Go on, sweetie, darling, coochie-coochie-pie.'

And then, appealing to his baser instincts, they all shouted, 'You can dress him up nice and sweet, and give him a new name. One that rhymes – why not Pedro the Potato-Peeler? Or Sergio the Super-Skin-Slicer?'

Luigi finally agreed, raising Sergio's basic salary by 10 per cent and putting him on an extra 20 per cent bonus per night, according to the number of extra customers he would attract into the restaurant by sitting next to the window magically rolling the skin off the potatoes.

He dressed him up in yellow, his favourite colour. 'Always reminds me of the early spring flowers in my native Tuscany,' he said. But the whole initiative turned out to be a disaster. When it came to the bit, Sergio froze and failed to perform. 'I was a trussed-up turkey,' he said to Archie and Angelina, 'sitting there in that window like some kind of whore. My hand just refused to operate. I did everything I normally did, but my hand refused to move and when it did I managed to cut myself and the blood spurted all over the place and the potato itself flew out of my hand.'

And Angelina, who was there when it had all happened, would add, 'And landed right down Victoria's dress, giving her three perfect breasts. The guys at the peephole creamed themselves.'

'Poor Luigi was almost sacked,' Sergio would add, 'but I pleaded for him and took the rap, saying it was all my fault and mistake and that it had been my idea. So they agreed to retain Luigi as long as he took a 10 per cent cut in his salary.'

'Which he takes off Sergio's wages, the bastard,' added Angelina, 'mincing around saying that it was his fault, who's never done anyone any harm his whole life.'

Because they only had one night off a week, and worked from morning till night the rest of the time and were given cheap subsidised accommodation in endless small rooms above the restaurant, Archie managed to save quite a bit of money. Unlike some of the others who either drank or gambled, or smoked, or snorted, or injected their wages, Archie was reasonably abstemious, only drinking on his night out with Angelina and Sergio. He was offered cocaine and all the rest of it, of course, but was smart enough to know that those who accepted these offers lasted only a few weeks in the restaurant before they disappeared or were sacked.

If I'm going to get north of that Pole, I can't succumb to any weakness, he said to himself every day, though he knew fine that weakness was what actually drove him on. But maybe weakness was at the heart of every heroism. What's refusing a white powder compared to swimming up through the Hudson, or walking barefoot with your feet falling apart with frostbite through the Frozen North, or crawling, like that man in Australia, hrough the red-hot desert for thousands and thousands of miles? Aren't we all now supposed to sacrifice for the greater cause? Suffer the pain of paying off the National Debt and all that stuff. Kill our children again in the trenches. Pro patria mori, in the fiscal interest. Drake was in his hammock, and a thousand miles away. 'Captain art thou sleeping there below, an' dreamin' arl the time o' Plymouth Hoe,' he chanted to himself, from some dark cave in the back of his memory. Or was that someone else too? Who the hell was it? Abercromby? *Eabarcrombaidh*? No, no. He was some general somewhere else. Montgomery? No – he was much more recent. Corunna? No, that was the battle itself. Sir John Moore, was that it? He was briefly back at school: *Not a drum was heard, not a funeral note, as his corse to the rampart we hurried; not a soldier discharged his farewell shot, oe'r the grave where our heror was buried.*

Heroes. Glorious heroes all. Even Bobby McGee, who thumbed a diesel down. Where did they come from, these long-forgotten snatches, all jumbled up and mixed together, like crosswires, like a software – or was it a hard disk – crash?

'Never just go by your feelings,' Gobhlachan had once said to him. 'Never, ever. Don't trust them. Trust your mind, or your reason, or your knowledge, or your imagination. Or your God. But don't trust your feelings. They will lead you astray, lead you to believe that black is white or bad is right.' And he would then hammer the anvil once more. 'Know right from wrong and you won't go astray.'

As if any human was capable of knowing that. And this jaunt to the Arctic? He wasn't just going by his feelings, was he, driven along like a wisp of straw by the wind, like a sheep by a bad shepherd, or a cow by hunger? To fall into a ditch somewhere like a blade of grass. Trust your mind. Archie laughed. Mind? What mind? Wasn't he the dunce of the village who once – famously – had said that one and one must make eight because his father and mother had married and then had eight children? And he'd been dead serious, completely believing it because that was all he'd ever known of it, and had no idea why the teacher turned purple with rage and whacked him eight times eight with the belt continuing to bawl at him as he cried, 'That's sixty-four, lad! Eight times eight! Sixty-four! Hear me? That'll teach you to be smart before your superiors, boy.' Whack, whack, whack. No wonder these lads at Heathrow continually just bawled fuck, fuck, fuck, like magic words to protect themselves. Like an iron hoop or a druidic circle round their hurts.

He mentioned his dream one night in the pub to Angelina and Sergio and, of course, they thought that going to the North Pole to find the source of that infernal wind was as reasonable a fantasy as any other.

'Sounds fair enough to me,' said Angelina. 'Each to his own. After all, think of George's dream. Or Osama's. What a cave of mirrors.'

As luck would have it, Sergio's two brothers were both First Officers at sea, working the International Flag Ships, registered for tax purposes in Liberia, but free to roam the world. 'They'll take you as near as dammit to the North Pole,' Sergio told him, 'though not necessarily by a direct route. It depends on which trade they're dealing with. One month it's the Gulf, the next the Baltic, the next Australia. I worked ship myself for a while – peeling the potatoes, naturally – but could never hack it. Always seasick. Tried two voyages – one to Brazil and one up to Iceland, but sick is sick whichever side of the Equator or date line you're on.'

Sergio meticulously explained how it all worked.

'Being registered in Liberia, they are free from national industrial laws – and most safety regulations, I warn you – and can pick up and hire crews wherever and whenever they want, on whichever terms they want. That's why they're mostly Filipino crews. Dirt cheap. And the officers from the East. Increasingly from China. But they would hire you, especially with a nod from me. You just work your passage. Free travel. Free food – which is wonderful by the way, with these Indian cooks. And half a normal salary at the end of the voyage.'

'Half a normal salary? What's wrong with getting the full whack?'

'Only if you sign on for a full five years. After all, they know they're basically just taking you to the other side of the globe so as to jump ship. Their attitude is that any illegal immigrant ought to be damn happy with free transportation, free accommodation, free food and a walletful of decent money in return for scrubbing decks all across the Pacific.'

'But I'm not an illegal immigrant,' said Archie. The fool.

'We're all illegal,' Sergio laughed.

'I've got a fully paid-up British passport,' continued Archie. 'I can't see any problem with that, even if I need to go through Burma itself to get to the Pole.'

'Visas, man,' said Sergio, 'and passes. Do you think they grow on trees? These can also be provided. And any passport you want. Any citizenship you want. My brother Ludo is the real expert on that. Just let me know what you want to be – American, Canadian, Russian, Faeroese – you name it and I'll text him right now. It can all be arranged.'

'I don't need any of that complicated rigmarole,' Archie said. 'I could just fly to the North Pole tomorrow.' But no one listened. He was only arguing with himself. 'Why should I get caught up in all these ridiculous scams and slave myself thrice round the globe when I could just get there with one visit to the travel agent's?'

But would he? Had he learned nothing?

Angelina and Sergio just laughed. 'What!' they both shouted together. 'Do you mean to tell us that you're really just a little bourgeois shit at heart? That really, at the end of the day, what you want to do is not to discover the source of this north wind at all, but to stand there with a bloody digital camera cawing, "Oh yeah! Look at me, with my big stupid fat smile, standing here at Ice Station Zebra, thanks to Cold Arse Travels. I made it! Amn't I good! And I'll have my lasagna supper tonight at the local Holiday Inn!" No way José! Do you think that's what Robert E. fuckin' Peary did, whom you're always going on about? Do you think that's what Captain Robert Falcon Scott did at the other end of the universe? Discovered the known universe thanks to Cold Arse But Warm Heart Travels?'

They were right, he knew they were. And they knew he knew, and all that stuff. So he asked Sergio to text his brothers, and within twenty minutes the whole deal was done. They were at that moment sailing west from Greece with a cargo of olives and other unnamed fruits, and due at Tilbury docks on the Tuesday morning. If he was ready at Station J at noon on the Wednesday, they would sail that afternoon, with Archie as a Canadian citizen, for Ludo reckoned that was by far the best way, for he'd once heard that there was actually a street in Toronto called North Street, which if you kept following it would eventually bring you out, in a straight line, at the Arctic Circle itself.

5

SO BY WEDNESDAY evening, as the sun set in all its redness to the far west, Able Seaman Archibald Grierson was sailing eastwards, leaving the jangling bells of Westminster in his wake.

He'd lived long enough near the sea to know that if the sun was setting behind you and you were moving away from it, you must be heading east, and had also been long enough in school to know that Canada, unless of course you were sailing by China way, lay west of Britain.

He also knew very well that to go west sometimes you certainly needed to go directly east first, but nevertheless he raised the issue with First Officer Ludo, who just told him to keep his head down, remain calm and keep scrubbing the decks.

'You have absolutely nothing to worry about,' he said, patting his breast pocket from where the false Canadian passport had emerged with a flourish earlier on. 'We're picking up cargo in Marseilles first, then we'll see where we go from there.'

The days were cold and windy going through the Channel, though that didn't stop the Head Bosun – a Russian called Bronowskielchev whom they all called Brawn – from driving them out on to the decks to scrape and clean and paint and tie and untie and shackle and unshackle all kinds of ropes and irons and doors and hatches and ladders. 'You see, as long as the outside looks all clean and neat and new and tidy they can get away with anything,' the crew muttered, knowing the whole truth of the thing, or at least their own part in the lie of it.

So when the sun burst through the clouds on the morning of the third day as they turned left – yes, the crew knew fine that was called port – and entered the Mediterranean, the ship sparkled white in the dazzling sun and you could see the tourists standing up high with their binoculars on the Rock of Gibraltar, peering down on the fine ship as she steamed by. Some even waved flags, in the forlorn hope that someone of importance – maybe even royalty – was on board.

Ludo played to the galleries by dressing up in his full officer's outfit, all white epaulettes with gold braid and a sparkling peaked hat fringed with royal blue flashing in the Mediterranean sun. He even saluted as he passed the crowds, and all that was needed was a twenty-one-gun salute to finish off the entire charade.

Most of the crew went to the brothels in Marseilles after unloading, though Archie just stayed on board. Not for any moral reason, nor because he wouldn't fancy a rough whore as much as the next sailor, but simply because he feared that the French police (as if they didn't have anything better to do) might nab him and take his false passport away. 'To tell you the truth, the Marseilles police don't give a shit what kind of passport you have, if you have one at all,' Brawn said to him, but still Archie stayed aboard.

Instead, he hid his passport deep inside his kit-bag and sat on it on deck during his hours off, watching the tour-boats go backwards and forwards between the dock and

Château d'If in search of the ghost of Edmund Dantès. The only other person who remained on board was Brawn, who sat opposite him on the capstan smoking – you've guessed it – Capstan cigarettes.

'Only get them in Russia,' Brawn said, 'this kind. In Vladivostok. Gregoria make them special for me. Twice-strength. Afraid of going fuck fuck?'

'No,' said Archie. 'Just that I don't want to go ashore. I'm happier safe here.'

'You never safe,' Brawn said, inhaling. 'No one ever safe.' He lit another cigarette while still inhaling the first one. 'This not safe,' he said. 'I'll die of this. Kaput. But if not this, then something else.'

'Sometimes it's safe,' Archie said. 'John Goblin used to smoke. One hundred a day. Lived till he was eighty!'

'John Goblin?' asked Brawn. 'Who's he?'

'Another Russian,' lied Archie. 'A big man. Strong. Able. Heroic. Like you. Live forever.'

This time Brawn laughed. 'No one live forever. Not even Ambromovitch despite his oil and football.' He smoked the two cigarettes together. 'Two two make four,' he said, blowing huge smoke-rings out of his mouth, both nostrils and his ears. 'From arse too. But you not see that,' said Brawn, though Archie could swear he saw huge smoke rings emerge from up Brawn's trousers. 'You know song?' Brawn asked.

'What song?' Archie asked.

'Smoke Song', Brawn said and began singing in a beautiful baritone voice,

'Thus must I from the smoke
Into the smother
From tyrant Duke
unto a tyrant brother.'

He blew the inevitable rings from all quarters. 'I can blow smoke any time,' he said. 'Just like Monsieur Pompadour.

'Where you from anyway?' he asked Archie. 'Not that passport-from,' he added. 'Real-from.'

'Oh,' said Archie, 'from far away.'

Brawn laughed. 'Of course. We all from far away,' and continued singing,

'But the majestic river
Floated on out of the mist
and hum of that low land
Into the frosty starlight.'

'Where you going to?' he then asked.

'North of North Pole,' said Archie. He could see Brawn really enjoyed the answer.

His eyes smiled.

'Hah! Where we're all going. North of the North Pole. You're very funny. Your name isn't Stalin?' And he suddenly darkened, like one of those quick stormy days from way back home. 'Vissarionovich Dzhugashvili killed the whole world,' he said. 'That's why I smoke.' And he blew ten enormous rings of smoke right out of the back of his trousers. They rose one after the other in loops into the air. 'I'll get him yet,' he said, and sang,

'Like as the armèd knight
Appointed to the field
With this world will I fight
And faith shall be my shield.'

'You're a great singer,' Archie said. 'You should be touring the world.'

'Am touring the world,' said Brawn. 'Round and round and round and round.'

'Were you a professional singer? An opera singer? The Bolshoi...?'

Brawn smiled again. 'I like you, boy. An opera singer! The Bolshoi! Do you want me to do a ballet or something? Like Nureyev? To keep your Russia alive for you? Next thing, you'll be speaking of Dostoevsky. Or the great dreamer himself, Count Leo.' And, fulfilling all expectations, he released a whole series of ballet figures out of all the orifices and sent them dancing and swirling and pirouetting all over the blue bay to Château d'If.

He suddenly went quiet again, and clear and still and pure, just as the skies would go after the storm and said in clear English, 'I was a university professor. Professor of Music at the Moscow Conservatoire. Youngest Professor of Music in the whole world. Just nineteen years of age. But I wrote this symphony – I jokingly called it *Smoke Gets in Your Eyes*. It was all about Stalin and the purges, of course. In the symphony everyone was blind in the mist and smoke.'

Right at that moment, they heard the sound of the returning taxis, the horns all hooting, and the sailors – or at least those of them who'd returned – leaping out of them and running up the gangway like kids after playtime.

Brawn stood up and for the first time Archie recognised how old he was. It was all perfectly possible. History is not all that old. As Gobhlachan used to say, just a minute's worth.

'Do you know,' Gobhlachan would say as the sun was sinking, 'that the sun is made new every morning? You know yourself it melts every night it enters into the water. But over on the other side, behind the mountain, a new one is made out of the fragments of all these shooting stars that fall from the sky all night.'

Archie once dared to ask him who gathered the fragments up and turns them into a new sun but Gobhlachan just laughed and told him, 'God, of course. Who else could gather up the fragments of the firmament?'

Within an hour they were sailing out of Marseilles, again heading east.

'Istanbul,' Ludo said. 'These things we picked up here in Marseilles have to be dropped off there. We pick up a different cargo there and make for Cairo. We've nothing booked from there but something will turn up. Likely we'll head down the Gulf to pick up some crude oil to take down to Australia.'

'Italy,' someone said to Archie, vaguely indicating to the left where a long strip of whitish land shimmered in the haze. Once, he'd seen porpoises fill the entire Minch, their tails fanned out all the way to Vatersay. 'If you sit on one,' his father had said, 'it will take you all the way to America.'

They were all back at their duties, scraping paint, lashing chains, polishing bulbs, repairing ladders. 'Like the good old days,' someone would mutter now and again.

'Ten years before the mast!'

'Lashed to the deck!'

'Land ahoy!'

'Convict ships!'

What Archie found remarkable was how predictable the whole unpredictable voyage became. Each morning, as if their lives were scripted, they would all return to their daily liturgy, scraping and painting and tying and unravelling and fixing. Each had his own curses, moans and hopes which he repeated daily as the ship travelled right across the globe, from Marseilles to Istanbul to Cairo to Aden to Muscat to Bombay to Sumatra to Freemantle to Wellington, right across the gorgeous hot Pacific to Panama, up through the

Bahamas and at last to Toronto across the Great Lakes, where Archie finally left ship.

Once they'd unloaded the cars from Marseilles and loaded the spices and rugs from Turkey and Afghanistan, the same thing happened in Istanbul as in Marseilles: everyone on board, except for Brawn and Archie, departed for the whorehouses, and while they were all gone the two of them sat on deck, this time under the shade of an awning of washed shirts.

'Some heat in that sun,' said Brawn, again expelling cigarette smoke all over the place. 'Do you think,' Archie began, 'that the sun gets wet when she sinks into the water?'

'No,' said Brawn. 'The sun is far too clever to drown herself.

'The ocean is just as wise,' he continued. 'She just divides, as the Red Sea once did, and lets the sun safely though to the other side.'

Explosions went off in the distance. The sun glinted on the church domes and on the mosque minarets.

'Brass or gold?' Archie asked.

'Oh – gold,' said Brawn, 'as in heaven itself. 'Why,' he asked, 'are you going to the North Pole?'

The question was so direct and simple that it frightened Archie. So he replied equally simply.

'To find the hole. The hole where the wind comes from.'

'The hole of death,' Brawn said. 'That's what you're trying to block up. And it's worth trying. Oh, it most surely is.' And he resumed the conversation broken the other day by the returning sailors in Marseilles. 'Do you know, they had killed everyone by that time anyway. My parents and my two sisters. Not that another four made much difference amongst the fifty-four million. The hole was so big that it could have swallowed the whole world, and still you wouldn't see the bottom. They didn't like the music anyway, and so sent me north. North! Hah!' he laughed. 'And by the time I came back, everywhere was north.' He paused, drawing breath. 'But it's worth it. Even though the hole was so deep that they couldn't fill it, they had to stop eventually. And do you know why?' Archie didn't say anything. 'Because the man with the spade finally fell in himself. The hole swallowed him too. Even though he left his spade.'

He lit another cigarette.

'Do you know they used to make cigarette papers out of the prisoners' skins? My smoke rings are only rings of remembrance. Dealing with grief through black humour. Famous as we are for our black cigarettes. There were so many of them. It's like living at the bottom of a well, but unable to drown. Like the sun itself.' He spat. 'Bloody metaphors. As if they were any use. Though they're all we have.' He stood up, the sun glinting on his bald head. 'I'll be seventy-nine next month, but feel as strong as when I was nineteen. Stronger, in fact. I've swallowed so much water. My heart is now made of liquid. I think I am condemned to live forever.' He laughed. 'There was an old man in my village when I was small. It was snowing. Everyone was starving. And do you know what he did? Climbed the highest mountain nearby, made a snowball and rolled it down the hill. It caught one hundred and one rabbits on the way down, which kept the whole village alive that winter.' He smiled. 'No point in telling a lie for the sake of a single rabbit.'

And there, under the hot Istanbul sun, Archie wanted to gather up the fragments of the stars and create a new sun.

'But your music,' he said. 'And all this.' As if he could restore Brawn's life with words. Or any of the other millions. As if by shouting 'Hurrah for Kintail' or 'Abracadabra' or rolling a snowball Brawn would stand once more on the orchestra podium, baton in hand, waiting for the graves to open. With a small pebble and a sling, David killed the Philistine.

The sun was setting and Istanbul was ablaze with its glory, the golden domes and minarets now all red. What better place for Brawn to settle down than here in this cradle of civilisation, amongst these Byzantine glories? But this was like every other port; this too was no country for old men: down in the tourist cafes in the squares Archie and Brawn could even then see the young in one another's arms.

'An aged man is but a paltry thing,' Brawn recalled, 'a tattered coat upon a stick.' And because English wasn't his mother tongue, it came out all broken and tattered, and ragged. Brawn looked out over the blazing city and said: 'Istanbul, Constantinople. Constantinople, Istanbul.' And releasing four perfect smoke circles from every orifice, said, 'Byzantium.' The rings rose into the evening sky like diminishing sacrifices.

The sun had now completely set and the city was suddenly bathed in that soft afterglow which brings on melancholy just before the night lights begin to sparkle. Archie watched Brawn standing by the ship's rail, like a man being gathered into the artifice of eternity. He stood like a woodcut out of the *Arabian Nights*, all noble and numinous and far away, and Archie knew that he was looking at Byzantium for the last time ever.

'Fire,' Brawn said. 'Look – pyres.'

Archie raised his eyes to the distant hills outside the city walls where Istanbul stretched into the mountains, where faint smoke could be seen rising into the night air from the small fires lit by the nomads who still survived in the old way out on the edge of the desert. Archie could smell peat smoke.

The brothel crew returned and the voyage continued, down through the Aegean and across to Port Said and the Gulf of Suez. In their off-hours they sat high in their bunks watching satellite television: news channels showing pictures of the very countries they were passing – the tented plains of Palestine, the severed oil-wells of Iraq, the thousands chanting in Enghaleb Square in Tehran. Tiger Woods was back on the seventeenth green discussing with his caddy whether he would use an iron or a wood for the approach shot. On yet another channel the Rolling Stones were playing, for the first time ever, in Red Square. 'Little Red Rooster', they wailed.

The voyage was both mundane and epic. That daily sea, and a different port every five days or so to discharge or upload all kinds of legal and illegal cargoes. It was routine and repetitive, even though the goods and events themselves were mind-boggling: transporting a whole group of young girls designated for prostitution, from Indonesia to Australia; fighting off pirates in the Sumatran Sea; rescuing fifty Nepalese off a raft in the middle of the Pacific; taking a band of guerillas from Bombay to Sri Lanka; guns and cocaine and all kinds of other weird and wonderful goods from one small corner of the earth to the other.

They became accustomed to it not because they were indifferent to the marvels nor because they were bowed into submission, but because the world they moved in was fluid. One day, this side of the International Date Line; the following day, forwards, or backwards, in time. One day, the sea boiling under the sun's rays; the next, the sea heaving in the middle of a monsoon.

Nature itself was erratic, and what was human kind and their ways but a mirror of nature? Different nations, different ports, different oceans, different cargoes and different people, but the one boat, with Ludo in his uniform up ahead, Brawn on the capstan, and Archie and the crew on their knees, scrubbing, with one eye on the horizon.

They claimed it was a gift. The gift of song which had, supposedly, kept sailors alive since the days of Noah himself. One evening at the forge an old woman had arrived with a broken cradle. 'I'll repair it for a song,' Gobhlachan had said, and as she sang the fragments of a lullaby the broken wood was transformed again into the Bethlehem crib, ready for the Christmas mass. 'A coin can take you a short distance,' the old woman had said. 'But a song can take you across the world.'

How beautiful everything was in song. No island was lovelier than home, and how sweet the day of return. But meantime, farewell and adieu unto you Spanish ladies. How easy it was now, Skyping from the South China Sea, while the former sailors studied the headlands for favourable winds. 'My, it's calm today!' '*Breac a' mhuiltein air an adhar; latha math a-màireach*' – A dappled sky today; a good day tomorrow. The highest mountain in the land is oftenest covered with mist. The owl is mourning, floods are coming. And a man had once said to him, 'The North Wind is cold no matter which direction it comes from.'

But Archie knew this: by the time he had crossed the Pacific he'd never looked better. Brown and sinewy, with the proverbial muscles in those proverbial places which he didn't even know existed, by the time they were sailing north-west through the Tropic of Capricorn he resembled a model old-fashioned sailor. If they could only see him now, these people back home, all brawny and tanned as he was, the very model of a man before the mast, even though the ship was all cylinders and hatches and electronics with not a mast in sight. Swarthy like Fionn MacCool himself, no one would recognise him now if they saw him:

'Who's that huge hero,' they would say, 'that giant over there felling all the trees with one sweep of his hand?'

How he would shame these part-time sailors now, these lobster and creel fishermen who all thought they were Neptune's warriors just because they could don oilskins and haul a few fat oysters in a trawl. Worse still were those in the North Sea, being helicoptered backwards and forwards once a fortnight from Aberdeen then lying in air-conditioned bunks, pretending when they came home and scoffed their pints in the pub that they were out there daily battling the elements, single-handedly drilling for oil in the depths of the North Atlantic. If truth be known, as he'd always known, thought Archie, the only real work these guys did was to lift a teabag occasionally out of a mug while they watched the computer screen detailing where, at that precise moment, the crude oil was actually flowing down through the pipes to St Fergus.

Which was not to say that it hadn't been heroic at one time: after all, someone had to be Buzz Aldrin. Someone had to be second, just as someone had to dive down at first to the very bottom of the sea with a helmet on his head and a tank on his back and dig beneath the rocks. But all that was a long time ago, before the heroes all died, and Archie knew fine that the oil industry now was a mere mechanical exercise, shifting keys on the computer, adjusting flows technologically, releasing or retaining oil according to the whims of the world's financial markets. Though such could also be heroes, even at their computers: for there is no greater hero than the financial wizard, who can make the world flow or cease.

But the day will come, thought Archie, when we'll all be back there, scrabbling around, trying to find a single peat for the fire, or a branch of twig from the shore, or some heather to light underneath a pot in which to make a bit of rabbit stew, and survive. How small his own peat-bank really was: twenty tiny sacks of crumbling moss on your back, and that was it. So he told himself this story.

There was a hero once. A king over Lochlann who had a leash of daughters. They went out one day to take a walk, and along came three giants and lifted the daughters of the king off with them, and there was no knowing where they had gone. Then the king sent word for the storyteller and he asked him if he knew where all his daughters had gone.

The storyteller said to the king that the three giants had taken them with him, and that they were in the earth down below, and that there was no way to get them but by making a ship which would sail on both sea and land. And so it was that the king sent out an order that anyone who could build a ship which would sail on both land and sea would get his eldest daughter in marriage.

In a poor corner of the kingdom there was a widow who had a leash of sons, and one day the eldest said to his mother, 'Cook for me a bannock, and roast a cock. I am going away to cut wood so as to build a ship that will go and find the daughters of the king.'

His mother said to him, 'Which would you prefer – the big bannock with my cursing, or a little bannock with my blessing?'

'Oh, give me the big bannock,' he replied, 'for it will be small enough by the time I build the ship!' So he got a bannock and went away.

He arrived where there was a great wood and a river,

and there he sat at the side of the river to eat the bannock. A great monster came out of the river, and she asked him for part of the bannock. He said that he would not give her a morsel, that it was little enough for himself. So he ate the bannock and began cutting the wood, but every tree he cut down grew again instantly, and this went on till night-time came.

He went home mournful, tearful, blind sorrowful.

His mother asked him, 'How did it go with you today, son?'

He replied, 'Terrible. Every single tree I cut down grew back up instantly again.'

A day or two after this, the middle brother said that he himself would go, and he asked his mother to cook him a cake and roast him a cock, and in the very way it happened to his eldest brother, so it happened to him. The mother said the very same thing to the youngest one, and he took the little bannock. The monster came and she asked for a part of the cake and the cock.

The young man said, 'Certainly.'

When the monster had eaten her own share of the cake and the cock, she said to him, 'I know full well why you are here, but for now go back home. Come back here, however, in a year and a day, and the ship will be ready for you then.'

And so it happened. At the end of a year and a day, the widow's youngest son went and he found that the monster had the ship floating on the big river, all fully equipped. He sailed away then with the ship, accompanied by a leash of gentlemen, as great as were in the kingdom, who all joined the voyage so as to try and marry the daughters of the king.

They were but a short time sailing when they saw a man drinking a river that was there. The youngest son asked him, 'What on earth are you doing?'

'I am drinking up this river,' the man replied.

'Well, you'd better come with me,' the youngest son said, 'and I will give you food and wages, and far better work than that.'

'I'll certainly do that,' the man said.

They had not gone far forward when they saw a man eating an ox in a park.

'What on earth are you doing?' the youngest son asked.

'I am here going to eat all the oxen in this park,' the man said.

'Well, you'd better come with me,' the youngest son said, 'and you'll get work, and wages far better than raw flesh.'

'I'll certainly do that,' the man said.

They went but a short distance when they saw another man with his ear to the earth.

'What on earth are you doing?' the youngest son asked him.

'I am here listening to the grass coming through the earth.'

'Come with me, and you'll get food, and better wages than to be here with your ear to the earth.'

They were thus sailing backwards and forwards when the man who was listening to the grass said, 'This is the place where the king's three daughters and giants went through the earth.'

The widow's son and the man who had been drinking the river and the man who had been eating the ox and the man who had been listening to the earth were let down inside a creel into a great hole which was there. Down at the bottom of that big hole they reached the house of the big giant.

'Ha! Ha!' shouted the giant. 'I know very well what you're seeking here. You are looking for the king's daughter, but you'll not get her unless you can find a man who can drink all the waters of the world like I can.'

So the widow's youngest son set the man who had been drinking the river to hold a drinking contest with the giant, and before he was half-satisfied, the giant burst.

Then they went where the second giant was.

'Ho! Hoth! Ha! Hath!' said the giant. 'I know very well why you've come here. You are looking for the king's daughter, but you'll never get her unless you have with you a man who can eat as much flesh as I can.'

So the widow's youngest son set the man who'd been eating the oxen to hold an eating contest with the giant. But before he was half-satisfied, the giant burst.

Then he went where the third giant was.

'Haoi!' said the giant. 'I know full well why you're here, but you'll not get the king's daughter unless you first of all stay here with me as my slave for a day and a year.'

'I'll certainly do that,' replied the widow's youngest son, and he sent the basket away back up with the three men and the king's three daughters. The three men then went with the three daughters to the king and told him that they had personally done all the daring deeds that were within their powers, which had freed his daughters.

When the end of a day and a year had come, the widow's youngest son, who had slaved for him all that time, said, 'Well, it's time I was going.'

The giant said 'Sure – now I have an eagle that will fly you up to the top of the hole and will give you your freedom there.'

So the giant set the eagle away with him, and gave the eagle fifteen pigs to eat while he was flying upwards, but the eagle had not reached halfway up the hole when she had eaten all the pigs and she returned back down to the bottom again. Then the giant said to the youngest son, 'You'll therefore need to remain with me another year and a day, and then I will release you.'

When the end of that year came he sent the eagle away with him, but this time giving him thirty pigs to eat on the way. Certainly this time they reached further than before, but three-quarters of the way up the eagle had eaten all the pigs and whirled back down to the bottom of the cave.

'You must,' said the giant, 'stay with me another year, and then I will send you away.'

The end of that year came, and the giant sent them away, with sixty pigs for the eagle's meat, and when they were at the very mouth of the hole the pigs were all eaten and she was going to turn back, but he tore a steak out of his own thigh and gave that to the eagle, and with one spring she was on the surface of the earth.

At the time of parting, the eagle gave him a whistle and she said to him, 'If you ever get into any difficulties, whistle and I will be at your side.'

He did not allow his foot to stop, or empty a puddle out of his shoe, till he reached the king's big town. He went where there was a smith who was in the town and he asked the smith if he was in want of a gillie to blow the bellows. The smith said that he was.

He was but a short time with the smith when the king's big daughter sent word for the smith.

'I am hearing,' said she, 'that you are the best smith in the town, but if you will not make me a golden crown, like the golden crown I had when I was with the giant, your head shall be cut off.'

The smith came home sorrowfully, full of lament, and

his wife asked him his news from the king's house.

'There is but poor news,' said the smith. 'The king's daughter is asking that a golden crown shall be made for her, like the crown that she had when she was under the earth with the giant. But what do I know about that crown. Nothing! How can I make something out of nothing?'

The bellows-blowing gillie spoke up. 'Don't you worry about that. If you get me enough gold, I won't be long making the crown.'

The smith got the gold as he asked, with the king's order. The gillie went into the smithy, and he shut the door; and he began to splinter the gold asunder, and to throw it out of the window. Everyone who passed by gathered up a fragment of the gold which the gillie was flinging out the smithy window. He then blew his whistle and in the twinkling of an eye the eagle appeared.

'Go,' he said to the eagle, 'and bring here the golden crown which is above the big giant's door.'

The eagle went, and soon returned with the crown between her claws. The gillie gave the crown to the smith, who went so merrily, cheerily with the crown to where the king's daughter was.

'Well,' said she, 'if I did not know that such is impossible, I would think that this is actually the crown I had when I was with the giant.'

The king's middle daughter said to the smith, 'Well, you will still lose your head if you won't make for me a silver crown just like the one I had when I was with the giant.'

The smith took himself home in misery. His wife rushed out to meet him, expecting great news of praise, but all she heard was this new tragic news. But the gillie again came to the rescue, saying that he would make a silver crown if he got enough of silver. The smith got plenty of silver with the king's order. The gillie went and did as he did before. He whistled; the eagle came. 'Go,' said he, 'and bring here to me the silver crown which the king's middle daughter wore while she was with the giant.'

The eagle went, and she was not long returning with the silver crown. The smith went merrily, cheerily with the silver crown to the king's daughter.

'Well then,' said she, 'it is marvellously like the crown I had when I was with the giant.'

The king's young daughter said to the smith that he should make a copper crown for her, like the copper crown she had when she was with the giant. The smith now was taking courage, and he went home much more pleasantly this time. The gillie began to splinter the copper and to throw it out of each door and window, and all the poor people from throughout the district gathered to collect the copper as they had already gathered the gold and silver.

Once again he blew the whistle and the eagle was instantly at his side.

'Go back,' he said 'and bring here to me the copper crown which the king's youngest daughter wore when she was with the giant.'

The eagle went and was not long returning. The eagle gave the copper crown to the gillie, who gave it to the smith. The smith went merrily, cheerily and he gave it to the king's youngest daughter.

'Well then,' said she, 'I would not believe that this was not the very crown that I had when I was with the giant underground, if there was a way of getting it.'

The king said to the smith that he must tell him where he had learned such crown-making, 'for I did not know that such a man as skilful as you lived within my kingdom.'

'Well then,' said the smith, 'by your leave, oh king,

it was not I who made the crowns, but the gillie I have blowing the bellows.'

'I must see this gillie,' said the king, 'so that he can make a crown for myself.'

So the king ordered four horses and a coach, that they should go and seek the smith's gillie. And when the coach came to the smithy, the smith's gillie was smutty and dirty, blowing the bellows. The king's horsemen came and asked for the man who was going to look on the king.

The smith said, 'That's him over there, blowing the bellows.'

'Look at the sight of him,' they said, and they went over and grabbed him by the scruff of the neck and threw him head-first into the coach, like a dog.

They weren't far on their journey when he blew his whistle. The eagle was instantly at his side.

'Get me out of here and fill it with stones instead,' he said to the eagle, and the eagle did just that.

The king was outside his castle, waiting for the coach to arrive, and when he opened the door of the coach, he was almost killed by the quantity of stones that fell out on top of him. He ordered that the horsemen be caught and hanged for the offence.

But the king sent other horsemen with a coach and when they reached the smithy, the had the same attitude.

'Goodness,' they said, 'is this the black dirty thing the king sent us to get?'

They grabbed him and flung him into the coach as if they had hold of a turf peat. But they hadn't travelled far when he blew the whistle and the eagle was at his side and he said to her, 'Take me out of here and fill it instead with every dirt you can get.'

When the coach reached the king's palace, the king went

to open the door. All the dirt and rubbish in the kingdom fell about the king's head. Then the king was in a great rage, and he ordered the new horsemen to be hanged immediately.

Then the king sent his own confidential servant away to bring the smith's gillie to the palace, and when he reached the smithy he gently took the blackened, bellows-blowing gillie by the hand. 'The king,' said he, 'sent me to seek thee. Thou hadst better clean a little of the coal off thy face.'

The gillie did this. He cleaned himself well. Extremely well. And the king's servant took him by the hand and put him into the coach. They were but a short time travelling when he blew the whistle again. The eagle came, and he asked her to bring the gold and silver cloak that was by the big giant to him without delay, and in an instant the eagle had returned with the cloak. The gillie arrayed himself with the giant's gorgeous cloak.

And when they came to the king's palace, the king came out, and he opened the door of the coach, and there was the finest man the king ever saw. The king took him in, and he then told the king how everything had happened to him from first to last.

The three great men who were going to marry the king's daughters were hanged, and the king's oldest daughter was given to him to marry. And they made them a wedding the length of twenty nights and twenty days; and the storyteller left them there dancing, adding that – as far as he knew – they might still very well be dancing on 'till the end of today', as he put it.

How beautiful to have your own eagle. And what a fabulous challenge: to build a ship that would sail on both land and sea! Wasn't that what Gobhlachan had done all his life?

Made things out of next to nothing; materials which could transform themselves according to circumstance. Grass which became beds; stones which became houses; flotsam which became furniture. Carts which doubled as hen-houses; ploughs which then served as gates and bridges; horse-shoes which also protected from all evil. All was alchemy. Words of course into stories, and stories which bent and altered time and history. He had a tale for every occasion, though it may just have been the other way round: that, like a modern spin-doctor or ancient houngan, every occasion generated its myth.

By the time Archie had told himself this story, they were near their destination, having sailed through the heat of Panama and up through the eye of a hurricane between Puerto Rica and the Bahamas. They were in that beautiful segment of the North Atlantic which stretches from Florida right up to the Gulf of St Lawrence, passing all the great cities of the world on its way, from Jacksonville in the Deep South to New York itself with its great statue proclaiming all the liberty of the new stories.

The Statue of Liberty as the eagle of freedom. Or was it Gobhlachan, or Ludo, who still stood strong up on the high deck, or old Brawn himself who guided all the ropes through his own leathery hands?

Brawn was still there, as part of the vessel and indeed as part of the ocean and seas through which they sailed. He never left the ship. He didn't go ashore in Liberia or in Cape Town, nor in Panama nor even in New York.

'He's been sailing now for fifty years, non-stop,' Ludo said. 'Never takes a day off. Never goes home on leave. Do you know that Brawn has never actually set foot on land since the day Yuri Gagarin died?'

And Brawn himself spoke it all out as they sailed that

August evening up past the statue, heading for the St Lawrence. All the rest were down below, sleeping or watching telly. It was a clear, starlit night with New York bearing as many lights as the heavens themselves.

The maiden's outstretched hand, gloriously lit, reminded Brawn of Michelangelo's painting, and the fragments, like the helper's gold and silver and copper emerged.

'Adam,' he said. 'Finger. God.'

And everything was clear.

He was the man who drank the rivers and ate the oxen and listened to the grass. Who descended into the hole and confronted the giant. Who stayed for a year and a day and a year and a day and a year and a day. Who went down into the Gulag to labour thanklessly for the giant. Whose freedom was stolen. Who cut down the trees which instantly grew again, not because he'd refused to give the bannock or cockerel away, but despite it. Because the beast knew he'd grabbed the large bannock with his curse. And he spoke all of that out with clarity as they moved north up past Martha's Vineyard and Cape Cod with Boston shining to port in the starry night.

'But maybe, if truth be told, it was all the other way round,' Brawn then said. 'It was impossible for him to kill us all. For where one – or a thousand – or a million – died, another one – or thousand – or million sprung up to take their place. And where is he now, the Beast who reigned over the known world? Gone, like a wisp of smoke. Like a bad smell out of your arsehole. The thing is, Archie, the symphony always wins through in the end. The music always overwhelms the silence.'

And he began to cry. Huge drops of water, like rain on a winter's day, poured down Brawn's cheeks as he stood there gazing out at New England beginning now to turn a coppery-silver in the early dawning of the day. And he began to hum, a deep sweet music which neither of them could imagine existed. It was, of course, the first movement from his own great symphony, and as he sang the music Archie could do little else but go over to him and join him in the dance, and so they waltzed along the empty deck of the ship with Ludo up on the bridge looking down on them, smiling, while the stars blinked out and the sun rose, shining all white on the blue sea before them that was the Gulf of Maine, that would take them round *Alba Nuadh*, Nova Scotia, to the mouth of the St Lawrence and the final entrance to the North Pole itself.

6

NORTH STREET IN TORONTO turned out to be a figment, naturally. There had, of course, once been a North Street, which became Yonge Street, then Highway 11, and mythic references declare it to be the longest street in the world. 'Sure, if you start walking from right there you'll eventually end up at the North Pole,' the saying went, from old liars who sat on the pavement chewing tobacco and remembering stories of the gold rush from scores of years ago.

Which was true of anywhere in the world. 'Just start from here,' they say in Dingle in the west coast of Ireland, 'and walk straight, and eventually you'll emerge at the North Pole itself.' 'From here,' they say in Ankara – 'actually, to be completely precise about it, from that exact spot over at that side of the broken bridge where the old market starts.'

From Edinburgh, you walk south, down the coastal road through North Berwick and on to Northumberland, or alternatively inland down through these lovely Borders towns – Galashiels, Jedburgh, Hawick and on to Carter Bar, – where you can see the whole of England – and therefore the whole of the world – before you.

Despite Ludo's assertion, North Street – then Yonge Street, and now Highway 11 – was not one long, flat, straight road to the end of the cowboy film. It may one time have held the saloon and the leaning awnings and the girls in parasols waiting for their men to come back from the Yukon, but now it was a complex shopping centre with malls and escalators and lifts. A world going up-and-down as much as a-long.

No longer could men stand at the end of the long linear street shielding their eyes from the sun and see Ole Smokin' Joe, or maybe Dingo Johnny Blue, or perhaps even Buckskin Bill himself come straight out of the north, loaded with gold. Now they came texting out of the glass lifts in the sky, laden with virtual gold from the global mines.

But since he was there now, Archie knew fine that this was the final road north. Through the shopping precinct, right along the pedestrianised mall, past the elevators and the glass buildings to the other side, where the coffee-shops and the university quarters began, then through that to the Viscount Park which brought you out on the edge of the northern suburbs, which then led out on to Highway 11 and from there to the very top of the world.

He knew fine other highways did the same – he'd checked them all on the inter-net. Route 37, known as The Cassiar Highway, which took you from British Columbia to the Far North, or the famous Dempster Highway, which took you from Dawson City in the Yukon Territories right to the Arctic Circle, but these were not his predestined ones. These were other routes, other lovers, other places.

On this road, which he now walked doggedly, emerging from the far side of Viscount Park into the thinning suburbs, his own friends walked with him, not strangers. He could see the huge Ontario prairie before him, the corn blowing in the breeze, the wheat ripening. Gobhlachan and Olga and John the Goblin striding and riding and hirpling up ahead: he could already see Gobhlachan sitting on the next milestone, his legs dangling between the legend 'The North Pole: 580 kilometers'. John the Goblin stood by the roadside, rolling a fag, and out slightly west of him, right through the rolling prairies he could see Olga Swirszczynska with her string of horses weaving through the high wheat. There had never been any Clearances. Eviction never happened.

Others were on Route 37 and on the Dempster Highway, but here on Highway 11 was where Jewel was, her slim beautiful hands carving out a language of her own. He glanced behind him, where Angelina and Sergio and Ludo and Brawn walked, now wrapping their aquafoil Arctic Peak jackets around them, tightening them against the coming breeze, the sure onslaught which would come from the north once they entered the tundra and the cold wastes where nothing – absolutely nothing – lay between them and eternity.

Brawn, his bald head bent into the wind, passed him, racing onwards.

'At the very least put gloves on,' he heard Angelina say to Jewel, as the wind began to bite, and she pulled a pair of beautiful silk gloves out of the side pocket of her rucksack and slipped them on, continuing to gesticulate silently in the now falling snow. The flakes were diamond-shaped and fell in slow-motion swirls. They moved octagonally westwards, like fairies do in the early twilight, pretending not to hurry.

Their feet made no noise and left clear marks in the snow. Each of them gazed ahead at the beautiful whiteness. How could anything be so white? How could white produce so much other whiteness, white upon white upon white? Was there a factory producing whiteness up there, pouring it out from the assembly line, like steel or whisky or newsprint? Were these glittering snowflakes really the tears of God frozen on the descent to earth? This meteorological reality outwith the old smithy. This atmospheric vapour frozen into ice crystals and falling to earth in light white flakes, as the *OED* has it. And what is atmosphere? The gathered breath of all the angels of mercy, as old Angus Gunn of Lochinver once put it. This envelope of gases surrounding the earth, and other planet, or substance, as the *OED* again has it. And vapour? – that moisture or substance diffused or suspended in the air, and so the definitions went on and on and on, one tautology after the other, going round in endless circles mentioning 'moisture' and 'substance' and 'air', in ever-increasing druidic rings, as in the famous Book of Kells.

People passed by, going south – homewards – heads bent deep in their cagoules, burdened with loaded rucksacks. Jeeps and trucks and lorries and even buses roared by, smiling faces peering at them through the glazed windows. Brawn walked first, his head bent, his body straight, his feet sure. Always first, no matter the pace Archie went at, no matter how much Jewel and Angelina ran, no matter even that time Sergio found a pair of abandoned skis by the roadside and launched himself off into northern space at the speed of lightning. Brawn was still there ahead of them, marching onwards steadily, his huge body bent into the wind, cutting a furrow through it like an ancient plough, casting the snow banks to either side. All they had to do was follow Brawn.

One evening Angelina fell, exhausted by it all. She lay back in the snow, like the corpse of Ireland in history, like that time the millions lay in the ditches of Dingle and Kerry and Connemara, hallucinating about that last single potato, that last single wet and withered potato which was of course all rotten and non-existent inside, like the poison of nothingness which they still tried to eat, ravenously, to assuage the great hunger, where clay was the word and clay the flesh.

Somehow Archie managed to get down on his knees beside her and tried foolishly to persuade her to rise when she was beyond all rising. But he placed his arms behind her and raised her up and set her on his shoulders, convinced of the resurrection not just as a theology which would miraculously reassemble the dead from all the known and unknown quarters of the globe – those who had been atomised into a thousand million pieces at Hiroshima along with his grandfather, torn to shreds at Ypres – but as a truth which he could personally witness, if he could bear her long enough, far enough, to that place where all things could be made new. It had always been posssible.

Unexpectedly, there was a roadside motel right in the middle of that wilderness. It shimmered dark out of the white wasteland and they took it to be a mirage, even though Brawn stood in the middle of the whiteout pointing and shouting back at them, 'Hotel! Fire! Food! Sleep!'

Sure enough, the window panes really rattled, the door really creaked and slammed. Inside, an old Indian woman appeared bearing steaming blankets and jugs of boiling water, guiding them into the Arctic saunas which stretched right across the back of the motel, where clouds of vapour enveloped them.

They all stripped naked and climbed into the perfect luxury of the hot tubs, lying back in ecstasy as the warmth invaded their bodies and made them remember home, and forget Janet Leigh. What a long way to have come to remember home. That time the new pillows came, the brand new duck-feather ones which curved right into the nape of your neck when you lay down and smelt like hay on an autumn morn, like fresh bread out of the oven. That time he – Brawn, that is – played his one tour of the west and walked the sun-scorched pavements of Paris after the garret-rehearsals releasing music, like jazzy pigeons, through the fully-opened windows.

Even the snow seemed warmer when they went back outside, Brawn leading with renewed vigour, as if the silence between the movements had reminded him of his purpose. Occasionally, he glanced back over his shoulder to beckon the others on: the deep cello movement of Archie, Jewel's strings, Gobhlachan's percussion, and Olga and John the Goblin and Sergio like flutes between the snowdrifts.

A bald man playing electric pipes stood by the roadside in the far distance. They all expected a lament, of course, but soon the gorgeous sound of marches and strathspeys and reels filled the sub-Arctic air, causing them to increase their speed through the drifts, like men floating across a universe.

'I lost my breath,' the bald man shouted to them as they passed by. 'Don't have the lungs any more, but this invention is marvellous. Permits me to play the great tunes without drawing breath.'

And he played on. Archie recognised 'Father John MacMillan of Barra', 'Crossing the Minch', '*Dòmhnall Beag an t-Siùcair*' and 'The 79th's Farewell to Gibraltar', amidst the now fading glory.

John the Goblin came hirpling up from behind, tugging a man by the sleeve.

'Archie!' he shouted, through the rising wind. 'Archie!'

Archie glanced round, and beckoned him onwards with his head, without stopping.

'Archie!' panted the Goblin, now beside him, 'this is Joe – Yukon Joe, he calls himself. He got lost in the snow, but I said he could come with us. Will that be okay?'

Archie nodded into the snow and the three trudged on abreast, John the Goblin to his right, Yukon Joe to his left.

John the Goblin pulled a tiny machine out from beneath the sleeve of his jacket.

'Brand new,' he whispered to Archie – presumably, so that Yukon Joe on the other side couldn't hear. But maybe he'd really shouted and the wind had just swallowed the whole world of his words. 'See – you just press this button here, and the whole universe is at your fingertips. It's a Berry, an Arcticberry. It works under any conditions.' And he pushed and flicked several buttons and the tiny touchscreen lit up in an explosion of light. 'Fifty pounds is all it would cost you. The RRP is £150, so it's a real bargain. Tweets and all!'

Yukon Joe leaned over and instantly the Goblin, like a conjurer, made the palmtop disappear. But Yukon Joe now plucked out a beautiful gold pocket watch, which glittered in the blinding whiteness. With one tiny movement of his thumb, he flicked open the watch to reveal the magnificent face, with what looked like hands of pure silver within a circle of hour marks made of rubies and diamonds.

'My real name is Albert,' Yukon Joe shouted into the wind. 'That was before I hit gold. This watch is worth five million dollars, but there is one tragedy in my life – I never learned to read, or write, or tell the time.' He flashed the gorgeous watch up before Archie's eyes. 'So can you tell me the time? What time is it, my friend?'

Archie looked at the watch, which despite all its beauty was completely indecipherable to him. The hour hand appeared to be going forwards without ceasing, the minute hand going backwards, and the second hand swirling round to the point of invisibility. Archie, of course, had heard that magnetic fields sometimes shifted, sending compasses astray, so he connected the disarray to that geophysical reality, though (if truth be known) it was merely that the watch was broken.

Brèagha ach gun fheum – beautiful, but useless, as

Gobhlachan might have put it – and as he often did when presented with a gashed plough, or a cracked cart, or a splintered shoe.

Gobhlachan had once repaired broken things, thought Archie. Once upon a time. A long, long time ago, which seemed like an hour ago, a second ago, as on Yukon Joe's watch. When time had travelled backwards, not forwards. Was circular, not linear. Was he too merely going round in circles? Would he, in a minute, finally discover the North Pole, and actually only find Gobhlachan sitting there on a freezing anvil under a flag, hammering away? Were these folk with him mere hallucinations, mere memories or dreams? Brawn, striding ever onwards, up ahead. John the Goblin hirpling to his right, Yukon Joe flashing his iridescent watch to his left. Angelina over his shoulders. Sergio and Jewel and Ludo plodding on behind. Was he going crazy?

Really crazy, he meant. Not that metaphysic craziness connected to memory and imagination, but real woo-woo-wah stuff, real crying in the wind stuff, the bleating and empty chaos, the dissolution of all things, despair. The bedside clock clicking at 3.22 a.m. time. And he would then plunge into the melting waters, drown in a sea of floating ice, having mistaken it for the imagined green lawn of Chelsea, where he'd once walked through Hyde Park on his way to the only football international he'd ever attended, that time Scotland beat England 3–2 with Jim Baxter scoring the winning goal, from a penalty, if memory still served him right.

'There's a band of gold round them islands,' Gobhlachan used to say, referring to the fishing-grounds. 'A band of gold plundered by pirates from the east,' he would then add, referring to the east coast trawlers which had sailed in and swept all the fish in the world away. Always how they came, the pirates – from the east. The raiders from the far side.

From some other place. From the far side of the island. From the other side of the mountain. From outside the song. From the story which didn't belong to us.

'All the gold is gone too,' he heard Yukon Joe say. 'The only gold that is now left is black. Black gold.'

And maybe that's when it began to dawn on Archie that the hole to the north was connected to oil. Was an oil hole. A black hole. A golden hole. Maybe too that was the moment when that strange word 'ozone' came to him. The hole in the ozone layer. Maybe, he thought, the hole is actually up above, in the sky, and not down below, in the earth or snow?

So he began looking upwards, but of course the sky was as white as the earth beneath him.

What if the north wind came from out of a hole in the sky and not out of a hole in the earth? How could he then fling his jacket over it and cover it, as in the old story? Maybe it was out of his reach. Too high up for him. Too far away from him. Invisible and unattainable. In light inaccessible, hid from his eyes. And even if he were to fling his jacket so high, how could it ever cover a hole so big, and what would it hold on to anyhow? He could hardly expect a jacket peg or a coat hanger to emerge right out of the sky, could he? Oh to believe in the ram, even like Jacob, the deceiver. There's the ladder. Reach out. One. Two. Jump. The great leap of faith. A giant step for...

In the old story, you see, Archie – tired of the incessant north wind – sought to extinguish it. So he left home and travelled for several days and finally found the wind whistling out of a small hole just to the north of the North Pole. So Archie did the sensible thing: he flung his jacket over the hole, saying to himself, 'That'll sort that!'

And he tramped back home, telling all the world that he'd fixed the north wind forever. And he lay that night in his bed listening to the utter silence until he fell asleep. And when he woke in the morning there it was again: that thin low whistle, coming, without any doubt, from the north.

So his neighbours all laughed and scorned him and mocked him: '*Amadain* – Fool,' they called out to him, 'I thought you said you fixed that north wind? Going around here boasting how you'd covered it with your Harris Tweed Jacket! What's that then?' and they all cocked their ears theatrically, as if they needed to do that to hear a wind which was roaring down on them, right from the bitter frozen north.

'Ah but,' said Archie, smartly, 'you see, it was only an old jacket I had with me, and it had a few holes in it, and that will be what the wind is seeping through. If only I'd taken a new jacket with me – or even a coat,' he would say, 'that would really have done the trick. That would really have sorted it out. A brand new jacket or a great big overcoat. That's what I ought to have had!'

And they were silenced by his audacity.

But now, here – now that it was real – Archie really feared. He knew fine that not even his aquafoil Arctic Peak jacket would be sufficient. Even if he found the hole and it was small enough, he knew fine that before he could even turn away his aquafoil Arctic Peak jacket (with all its quadruple-insulation and five-fold anti-freeze polytetrafluoroethylene lining) would be blown to kingdom come, become yet another miniscule piece of non-biodegradable rubbish floating about the universe.

Myth was one thing, he knew, this was another. Maybe Brawn had the answer. He might – he surely would – know what to do.

Archie shouted, but Brawn marched relentlessly onwards, without even turning his head. There was no point, he knew, in asking John the Goblin or Yukon Joe: all they would do would likely be to try and sell him his own jacket.

So he stopped and waited, till Sergio and Ludo and Jewel caught up with him, their heads buried deep inside their hoods, bent into the wind. Try as he might, Archie just couldn't make out what Sergio and Ludo were saying, or trying to say, but Jewel's gloved hands moved in the blizzard, slicing this way and that, pushing snowflakes up, pressing floating drifts down.

'Don't worry,' she was saying, in her magic language. 'You just have to believe the old proverb which says that a bird's feathers grow as needed. If you'll need a jacket, you'll have a jacket, if you need a greatcoat, a greatcoat will be provided.'

Each moment has its solution, Archie thought. Is that what she's saying? *Nuair a thig latha, thig comhairle* – when the moment comes, counsel will come – as Gobhlachan never tired of saying. Foolishness, others said. Lack of foresight. Laziness. Stupidity. Trusting in Providence. The something-will-turn-up philosophy, as if you could feed off hot air and vague hopes. As if magic genies really existed, ready to pop out at any moment to fix your own disastrous dreams.

There is no magic jacket, Archie thought to himself, still pushing onwards. No ram will appear out of the thickets of this whiteout. No magic lamp. No magic wand. No magic feather. No talking cow which will lead me to the cave. No dragon's extracted teeth which will turn into an army of soldiers for me. Salvation from the outside. Miracle, not endeavour. Providence, not labour. Law. Grace.

How much the cèilidh house had been the inter-net cafe of the time. Walking to Gobhlachan's forge to log-on to the stories. Click Gobhlachan stories. And news and speculation. The similarity between fact and fiction, between story and science. And how they would all sit round the open terminal of the kiln fire, trawling through the myths, that amazing website sourced in Gobhlachan's head. In Gobhlachan's heart. Though, of course, he too was just trawling from ancient resources, harnessing the past.

And here Archie was now, nearing the source of the web, trampling through the snow to reach the invisible, to see if he could catch a glimpse of that spider who wove the web, silently moving backwards and forwards above the ether, leaving that thin trail behind him which then sparkled beautifully in the sun as if it had been woven for pure pleasure, when in reality it was but the arachnidan trace simply designed to capture insects as food. Though even that was miraculous, Archie thought. Imagine. That a spider could invent that.

He felt a pair of freezing-cold hands slip inside his gloves next to his own. Jewel entwined her fingers round his, taking him literally by the hands and leading him gently onwards, to her vision of God. This was no Eve, Archie knew, for despite all that other stuff about Satan appearing in the guise of light, and about Eve the Temptress – that silky, slinking, sensuous, sexy serpent – this Jewel was pure light, 'as pure as the light of the Gospel itself', as Gobhlachan used to say when he wanted to emphasise the complete truth of any tale.

And all of a sudden, there it was, glittering ahead. The snow had stopped and the stars shone in all their glory in the endless sky above and Archie could see the perfect arc of the North Pole, just as it had always appeared in pictures, blue and limpid and translucent, and as perfectly shaped as in the globe he'd once seen hidden inside the glass-fronted book cabinet in the teacher's study.

And then, out of the perfect silence, the noise started. The noise of motor engines and vehicles and machinery, up ahead, in this blue heaven. A vast convoy of cranes moved from left to right, followed by hundreds of articulated lorries on caterpillar tracks and thousands upon thousands of men driving backwards and forwards hauling all the world's machinery behind them: cogs and chains and cables and pistons and tubes and hydraulics and all the rest of the magic equipment which drills down into the heart of the earth – even the frozen earth – to draw up the liquid oil.

A man with the facial features of a Chinese, but with a slow Texan drawl, came up to Archie, doffed his cowboy hat and said, 'Howdy.' Really. He smiled broadly, extending a large, ungloved hand. 'Welcome boys,' he said to Archie and John the Goblin and Yukon Joe and Sergio and Ludo and Brawn and, smartly noticing that Jewel, despite her aquafoil Arctic Peak jacket, was a woman, lowered his hat even further, adding, 'And you too, Maaam. There's no discrimination going on up here, Maam. No siree.'

He whistled sharply and loudly and a jeep bearing two medics raced across the snow. 'Take that poor soul straight up to Med HQ.' The Chinese-Texan indicated the almost frozen Angelina, still borne like a lamb across Archie's bowed shoulders. 'She'll be right as right in no time.'

And off the medics sped with her, past the canteen and the sleeping-sheds.

'No one's ever died up here,' he said, 'and we don't intend to start that bad habit right now. 'My name's Ted,' he said, 'and if it's work you want, you've come to the right man, at the right time, in the right place. We start drilling in a month's time and we can use as many hands as we can get. All hands to the deck, as they say. Many hands make light work, as others say. And that's why we're here – literally to make lights work! Without us, the lights would go out all over the world. Hah hah.'

And that's what he really said – not a laughing sound, or even a kind of hah-hah-noise, but actually and literally, 'Hah hah.'

'That's why they call me Ted Hah,' he said without smiling, 'though my mother really was Chinese. Her name was Li Ha. Hah hah.'

And he really laughed, even though it seemed well rehearsed to Archie.

He led them to their sleeping quarters, showing them each into their own room.

'Comfort, folks,' he said, 'that's what it's all about. No crowded quarters here, folks. This is my motto: a bad sleep and work slips; a good sleep and work shifts. Compressed sleepers make crushed workers. We want you to be clean and free. Everyone with his and her own room. Even scented and with fresh flowers daily,' he said, smelling the sweet air. 'The flowers are flown in from California each morning.'

As he lay in his warm bed that night, Archie was aware of the dream. How comfortable this bed was. This was life, life in all its fullness. There was nothing like it. He would forsake the whole world for it. The laundered sheets smelt of pine.

Strange, how we always want to cage nature.

He could hear the sound of the drills going through the night. He had signed no contract, so why should he stay? He could depart – take his leave, as they put it in the old stories – in the morning. Surely he wouldn't stay just for the comfort and warmth? He would tear the world for what? For central heating. For a car under his backside, a sweet little bedside lamp, a washing machine for his wife's stockings?

But that was only a tiny part of it. The bourgeois conscience which had the luxury of choice. What about the poor of the world who had no choice? Was there any truth in the claim that they too were dependent on oil, upon the crumbs of the crumbs that fell from the rich man's table? Would the poor man starve twice over if the fat man grew lean?

But he knew that had nothing to do with it. The poor can do what they like. Let them starve twenty times over, as long as the lights glitter in Paris. No. They would ask him to sign a work contract in the morning, not for the sake of the poor, but for the sake of the rich. He would go a-drilling not for Africa's sake, but for America's. For his own sake. He would help find oil which would make gasoline for cars, and which would heat houses in Times Square. And Tiananmen Square. And every other square and hovel in the developed and undeveloped world.

And Archie's brief contribution to it wouldn't affect things that much: he would hardly make a wick for a lamp, when you thought about it. The harm – could you really call it destruction? – wouldn't amount to much, after all. For who, or what, was he anyway, in the large scale of things? One small, weak man – one little Archie, even if he had Brawn and Sergio and John Goblin and all the others at his shoulders.

He walked over towards the window. He spread the curtains and looked out at the heavens. A large, white bear stood yards away, looking at him. An Arctic hare sat in the snow a little distance behind the bear. All the stars that ever existed blinked above. He thought he saw a row of penguins marching past till he remembered that was at the other end, to the south, at the different Arctic called the Antarctic. Just as they call South Uist one island and North Uist another.

Maybe the two had met. Maybe both polar ice caps had now melted and all was one. Norway without the fjords. The magnetic fields had shifted and all was now north, or south, or neither.

How vast it all was out there. How wide and white and long. Eternal even – one endless whiteness after the other. In such immensity, surely a little, or even a lot of drilling would do very little damage. A drop in the ocean really. Only the removal of a single star from the vast and limitless sky. Only the taking of a single flower from the machair, the removal of a single shell from the shore, the subtraction of a solitary letter from the cosmic alphabet. When the village postie took a notion for strong drink, he too would just dump the letters and parcels under the nearest pile of stones. Nobody really missed them. And if anybody wanted them, they knew where to find them.

Archie could hear Brawn rumbling in the room next door. Apart from that, all was silence. The machinery had been set for the night and work was not scheduled to really begin till tomorrow. That much he'd learned from Ted Hah, who'd personally come round the sleeping quarters at bedtime, like Florence Nightingale: 'The show starts tomorrow. Night-night. Sleep tight. Don't let the bugs bite!' And off he went down the long hall, repeating his soothing words like a benediction.

The room was centrally heated and a brand new pair of pyjamas had been laid out for Archie on the heated rail beside his dressing cabinet. He was now still in his pyjamas, gazing out at the white world. Far to the north he could see the Pole Star itself, winking. False stars were stuck to the wall and ceiling which then illuminated for a while once you turned the light off.

Archie climbed back into bed and put the light out. The imitation stars were shining on the ceiling: stars with five points and crescent moons, all in different colours. An orange moon and a yellow one. A red one and a blue one. The Star of David. Archie lay back, his head on the downy pillow. Was this it – the source of the wind, the lion's den, the giant's awesome abode? In the warmth, beneath false stars?

How do you behave in the lion's den, he wondered? What do you do at the giant's table?

How do you sleep in the dragon's bed? Do you pretend? All the images – all the stories he'd ever heard – raced though his brain in kaleidoscopic sequence: George and the Dragon, Daniel in the Lion's Den, Goldilocks and the Three Bears.

Do you slay, or pray, or run?

He had no sword. Had he faith? Could he run?

He was tired. And old. And lazy. And it was unfair to rely upon his friends.

Be wily, he told himself. That was always the chief virtue. The thing that was praised. Craftiness. The greatest skill. Courage. Courage certainly, but cunning was more important. Never attack a giant head on. You stood no chance. Always find his weak spot, his Achilles heel – wasn't that the way they put it? Achilles, who found the tiny spot which made the invincible giant mortal. Right behind his ankle. The monster's hidden weak spot. For every monster had a weak spot. Sex. Greed. Ambition. Pride. Sloth.

There was a king over Èirinn once, who was named King Cruachan, and he had a son who was called Connal MacRigh Cruachan. The mother of Connal died, and his father married another woman. She was for killing Connal, so that the kingdom might belong to her own posterity.

He had a foster mother, and so Connal went to live in the home of his foster mother. He and his eldest brother were right fond of each other, and the foster mother was vexed because Connal was so fond of her big son.

There was a bishop in the place, and he died. And he desired that his gold and silver should be placed along with him in the grave. Connal was at the bishop's burial, and he saw a great big bag of gold being placed at the bishop's head and a great big bag of silver at his feet, in the grave. Connal said to his five foster brothers that they would go in search of the bishop's gold, and when they reached the grave Connal asked them which they would rather – go down into the grave or hold up the flagstone.

They said they would hold up the flag. So Connal himself went down into the grave and whatever squealing that they heard, they let go the flagstone and they ran off home. So there Connal was, in the grave on top of the bishop. When the five foster brothers reached the house, their mother was somewhat more sorrowful for Connal than she would have been for the five.

At the end of seven mornings, a company of lads went to take the gold out of the bishop's grave, and when they reached the grave they threw the flat flagstone to the side of the further wall. Connal stirred below, and when he stirred, they ran, leaving their armaments and their dress. Connal arose and took the gold with him, and the armaments and dress, and he reached his foster-mother with them. They were all merry and light-hearted as long as the gold and silver lasted.

Now there was a great giant near the place, who had a great deal of gold and silver hidden in the foot of a rock, and he always promised a bag of gold to any being who dared to go down into the hole inside a creel and get some. Many were lost in that way: when the giant would let them down and they would fill the creel, the giant would not let down the creel more till they died in the hole.

On a day of days, Connal met with the giant, and the giant promised him a bag of gold if he agreed to go down into the hole to fill a creel with the gold. Connal went down, and the giant was letting him down with a rope. Connal filled the giant's creel with the gold, but the giant did not let down the creel to fetch Connal, so Connal was stuck in the cave amongst the dead men and the gold.

When the giant failed to get any other man who would go down into the hole, he sent his own son into the hole giving him the sword of light in his lap so that he might see his way before him. When the young giant reached the bottom of the cave and when Connal saw him, he immediately grabbed the sword of light before he realised what was happening, and he took off the head of the young giant.

Then Connal put gold in the bottom of the creel, and he climbed in and then he covered himself with the rest of the gold and gave a pull at the rope. Up above, the giant drew up the creel, and when he did not see his son he threw the creel over the top of his head. Connal leapt out of the creel as it flew behind the giant's great black back, laid a swift hand on the sword of light which he'd taken with him and cut the head off the giant. Then he took himself to his foster mother's house with a creelful of gold and the giant's sword of light.

After this, one day he went to hunt on Sliabh na Leirge. He was going forwards till he went into a great cave. He saw, at the upper part of the cave, a fine fair young woman who was thrusting the flesh-stake at a big lump of a baby. And every thrust she would give the spit the babe would give a laugh and she would begin to weep.

Connal spoke, and he said, 'Woman, what ails thee at the child without reason?'

'Oh,' said she, 'since you are an able man, kill the baby and set it on this stake so that I can roast it for the giant.'

Connal caught hold of the baby, and he put the plaid he had on about the baby and hid the baby at the side of the cave. There were a great many dead bodies at the side of the cave, and so he set one of these on the stake, and the woman began roasting it.

Then was heard underground trembling and thunder coming, enough to terrify the life out of any living soul. So Connal sprang in the place of the corpse that was at the fire, in the very midst of the bodies.

The giant came and asked, 'Is the roast ready?' He began to eat, complaining, '*Fiu fiu haogrich*. No wonder your body is rough, woman. This child of yours is tough to eat.'

When the giant had eaten that one, he went over to count the bodies; the way he had of counting them was to catch hold of them by the ankles and to fling them over his head, and he counted them backwards and forwards like that three or four times, and as he found that Connal was somewhat heavier than the corpses, and that he was soft and fat, he took that slice out of him that stretched from the back of his head to his groin. He roasted this at the fire, and he ate it, and then he fell asleep.

Connal winked at the woman to set the flesh-stake in the fire. She did this, and when the spit grew white after it was red, he thrust the white-hot spit right through the giant's heart, and the giant was dead.

Then Connal went and he set the woman on her path homewards, and then he went home himself.

His stepmother sent him and her own son to steal the white-faced horse from the king of Italy, and they went together to steal the white-faced horse, and every time they would lay hands on him, the white-faced horse would let out a cry. Guards came out, and they were caught. They were imprisoned and their ankles put in tight, painful chains.

'Hey you, you big red-haired man,' the king said to Connal, 'were you ever in such dire straits as this?'

'Make the chains a little tighter for me, and a little looser for my comrades, and I will tell you,' said Connal.

The queen of Italy was looking at Connal. Then Connal said:

'Seven morns so sadly mine,
As I dwelt on the bishop's top,
That visit was longest for me,
Though I was the strongest myself.
At the end of the seventh morn
An opening grave was seen,
And I would be up before
The one that was soonest down.
They thought I was a dead man,
As I rose from the mould of the earth;
At the first of the harsh bursting
They left their arms and their dresses.
I gave the leap of the nimble one,
As I was naked and bare.
'Twas sad for me, a vagabond,
To enjoy the bishop's gold.'

'Tighten his chains well, and right well,' said the king of Italy. 'He was never in any good place. He has done great ill.'

Then his chains were tightened tighter and tighter, and the king said, 'You big red-haired man, were you ever in such dire straits?'

'Tighten my chains even further, but let a little slack with this one beside me, and I will tell you,' said Connal.

They tightened even further. 'I was,' said he:

'Nine morns in the cave of gold;
My meat was the body of bones,
Sinews of feet and hands.
At the end of the ninth morn
A descending creel was seen;
Then I caught hold of the creel,
And laid gold above and below;
I made my hiding within the creel;
I took with me the glaive of light,
The best thing that I ever did.'

They gave him the next tightening, and the king asked him, 'Now, were you ever in such dire straits, in such extremity as hard as this?'

'A little more tightening for myself, and a slack for my comrade, and I'll tell you that.'

They tightened his chains, and loosened his comrade's, and Connal said:

'On a day in Sliabh na Leirge,
As I went into a cave,
I saw a smooth, fair, mother-eyed wife,
Thrusting the stake for the flesh
At a young unreasoning child. "Then," said I,
"What causes thy grief, of wife,
At that unreasoning child?"
"Though he's tender and comely," said she,
"Set this baby at the fire."
Then I caught hold of the boy,

And wrapped my cloak around him,
Then I brought up the great big corpse
That was up in front of the heap;
Then I hear Turstar, Tarstar, and Turaraich,
The very earth mingling together;
But when it was his to be fallen
Into the soundest of sleep,
There fell, by myself, the forest fiend;
I drew back the stake of the roast,
And I thrust it into his maw.'

There was the queen, and she was listening to each thing that Connal suffered and said. And when she heard this final truth, she sprang and cut each binding that was on Connal and on his comrade and she said, 'I am the woman that was there.' And to the king: 'And thou art the son that was yonder.'

Connal married the king's daughter, and together they rode the white-faced horse home.

And as he lay there, telling himself that ancient story, Archie was encouraged. 'Hah!' he laughed to himself – and a real laugh it was, even though it has to be written down as 'Hah!' here, in just exactly the same way as Ted Hah's very different 'Hah!'

The giant was Capitalism, Archie knew, and the hole was where the bodies of the poor lay scattered in the Cave of Profit where all the gold lay. They were the ones daily sent down in creels to labour for the giant. They were the ones eaten alive. Roasted on the spits. Even their corpses consumed. And this, of course, was to be his job here: to go down daily in that creel to find the gold, and bring it to the surface. To dig for oil in this virginal landscape. To bring the fat baby up so that his blood could be used as fuel to feed the giant.

If he were Connal, what would he do? Run? Uh-uh. Forsake the contest? No way. Hide beneath the blanket, pretending the giant didn't exist? What was it all but a story anyway, of little use nowadays? A foolish pastime which belonged to the olden days when folk believed such nonsense? Even though the smell of roasting flesh was in their nostrils, even though they could hear the giant's rumblings, even though they could clearly see him on their computers? All that cynical blogging out there where no one believed anyone else.

And poetry! Remarkable how poetry caused Connal to be released. Believe that if you will, you fool. Dream on, MacDuff. As if that could happen! Oh aye. Pull the other one, son. You try that on the next time you're taken captive by al-Qaida. Just stand there and start chanting this to them – '*My love is like a red, red rose, that's newly sprung in June…*'

Archie listened to Brawn breathing steadily in the next room: like the soft breathing of a child. How thin the walls between beings. As long as you could hear someone else, you were alive. He was talking in his sleep. 'Snow. White. Soft.'

Archie recalled all the corpse-strewn caves he'd ever seen on television. Those earthquake-heaved streets of Port-au-Prince. The oiled beaches of Louisiana, and the long poisoning of the Niger Delta. The jutting elbows and knees and shoulders in Uganda. The black and white skeletons of Auschwitz. The giant's creel suspended halfway down in the deep-cast mines of New South Wales.

But he had no sword of light.

'Now, who had the sword of light,' he asked, 'in the story, I mean. Who had the sword of light?' And, of course, he remembered that the giant's son had the sword of light. Given him by his father. 'Ah,' said Archie 'So it was the giant himself who first had the sword of light!'

'What is it?' he asked himself. 'What is this sword of light?'

'Iron or steel,' he heard Gobhlachan say. 'Remember, son – iron and steel were so hard to come by, so anyone who had them was already halfway to victory. Anyone who had a gleaming sword was already well on the way!'

'But that was then,' Archie said. 'What is it now, though? What's the material which gives the giant the advantage now? What is it, Gobhlachan?'

But Gobhlachan was silent.

Wasn't that the entire point? Connal worked it out for himself. No manual. No exposition. No clues beforehand, except the stories he carried within himself. His mental knowledge of the giant. The death of his mother. A grasping foster mother wanting to kill him. Bereavement and fear. The bag of gold and the comfort and security it offered. A penitent banker laughing round every corner.

No clues as to the sword of light. Who made it, and how, and was there another of its kind? Was there a market for it, or was it kept secretly, hidden? Could you just download it? What could the sword do? That was the sword which could upwards and downwards, cutting the nine ties on its way across, and nine ties on its way back. It's just that the giant had it. And Connal managed to get hold of it.

What was it? Oil? Wealth? Knowledge? Power?

And to grasp it, Connal had to enter the cave. The cave of gold. With all the danger and sorrow it carried. Into the darkness. Where the stench of death lay. Lazarus, come forth.

Connal didn't just text or email the giant:

Dear Mister Giant – I hope you're well, and I'm very sorry to bother you, but it would be really lovely if you could – please – release those people you have captive in your cave.
PS *And the gold as well.*
PPS *Happy Christmas and a Guid New Year to yin an a'.*

But he was so tired, exhausted after such a journey. And Angelina almost dead on his shoulders, where was she? How was she? And Brawn – big, beautiful, courageous Brawn – forever marching on ahead. And the bed now so sweet and soft, the room so warm, the flowers so bright.

Yet all he wanted to do was sleep and none of that sword up and down stuff, and then that hot shower in the morning and the bacon and eggs, and keep his mouth shut and stay quiet and mum, and just go out daily to dig or drill or extract – whatever was asked of him – without raising any awkward questions, without being difficult and bolshie, without making trouble, without putting himself – and, for that matter, Brawn and Angelina and Jewel and Sergio and Ludo and John the Goblin and Olga and Gobhlachan and Yukon Joe and all the rest of them – at risk. At risk of being sacked, thrown on the scrapheap, turned out into the blizzard and snow, to fend for themselves again or die, alone, unwanted, uncounted in these endless Arctic wastes.

And who would give a damn?

The whole circus would just roll on anyway, without their futile, deadly gesture. What was the point? He was no Connal. And he settled lower into the duck-feathered pillow. To sleep, he thought. To sleep. To sleep. Perchance.

'Grip. Nail. Frost,' Brawn was saying in his sleep next door and as he drifted off to sleep Archie remembered his own wife and son endlessly sitting in front of the television, also ceaselessly channel-surfing.

'Maybe, really, I'm the giant,' Archie thought, as he finally fell asleep. All night he dreamed that someone had taken his wife and son captive and they were being held prisoner in two creels suspended halfway between the earth and the grave, between today and tomorrow.

7

HE WAS WOKEN in the morning by a quiet knock on the door, and a woman's voice saying, 'Good Morning, Mr Grierson.' A woman entered dressed as a bunny-girl, bearing a big hearty breakfast on a tray – fresh coffee and croissants with a basket of fruits.

'Sponsorship,' she said. 'You know how it is. The world's gone to rack and ruin if you ask me. You can hardly go to the loo nowadays without sponsorship. Here's your breakfast, thanks to Playboy Inc. The misogynistic bastards. But then it's a good wage, isn't it?' She put the tray down on his table. 'Oh – and I'd better say it,' she said. She smiled beautifully. 'Have a nice day.' She left, leaving the sweet fragrance of coffee in her wake. But then she opened the door again and stuck her lovely face back inside. She was covered in freckles. 'Oh – I'm Barbara. But you can call me Babs.' She waved her fingers. 'Cheers.'

That was only the bed-breakfast. After his second, real breakfast – ham and eggs and sausage and black and white puddings and mushrooms and all the rest of the cholesterol killers – he signed the contract as part of the Alaskan Oil Company Drilling Team, who had been given the franchise to explore The Great Northern Field, as it was known.

Big Ted Hah himself did the presentation for all the new workers hired: an all-gizmo, all-singing, all-dancing PowerPoint presentation which beautifully demonstrated, through remarkable figures and graphs and sliding photographic and video shows, how the Alaskan Oil Company Drilling Team, along with their partners, BP, Statoil, Ruskoil, Chinoil, ExxonMobil, Amoco, Conoco, Texaco and PetroCanada were involved in what he called the Great Project.

'A Great Project in a Great Petroleum Field from a Great Company with a Great Workforce!' he enthused, flicking one button after another, displaying oil wells in full flow, rigs sparkling like gorgeous Christmas trees, an African woman carrying wood on her head to light a fire, and an all-white Rolls-Royce purring down through some mythic sleepy Swiss Village. 'Fuel,' said Ted, 'that's what binds us all together. Oil and wood and gas, keeping the world turning.

'Contentment,' continued Big Ted Hah softly, as he pressed the PowerPoint slides: happy Chinese children eating from full rice-bowls; Putin playing ice-hockey in Siberia; Italian women pouring waterfalls of spaghetti on to plates; old Highland men in kilts driving through whitewashed villages in their Fordson Majors. 'The whole world on the move,' declared Ted. 'This is not Capitalism with a Capital C, but capitalism with a small c and Co-operation with a Capital C! This has nothing to do with Oil Companies and Profit,' he purred, warming to the Great Theme, 'but Everything to do with Developing the Global Economy, Protecting the Environment, Ensuring the Wellbeing of All World Citizens, Caring for the Poor, Shielding the Weak, Restraining the Strong. As the Great Old Testament Prophet Isaiah put it, in far more mellifluous words than I could ever put it: "The Lord Himself has anointed me to preach Good News to the Poor. He has sent Me to bind up the Brokenhearted, to proclaim Freedom for the Captives, and Release for the Prisoners, to Proclaim the Year of the Lord's Favour and the day of Vengeance of our God, to Comfort All who Mourn, and to Provide for those who Grieve in Zion – to Bestow on Them a Crown of Beauty Instead of Ashes, the Oil of Gladness, instead of Mourning, and Garment of Praise instead of a Spirit of Despair. You will be called Oaks of Righteousness, a Planting of the Lord, for the Display of His Splendour!"

'That is why,' he added with a tearful flourish, 'we will be calling the oil that comes from this Pioneer Field "The Oil of Gladness". Now, all I say, to All of you, as we enter Together on this Great Venture, is what the Great Roman said when the legions set out to conquer the world: "Each man is the smith of his own fortune; but together, we are the forge of the world!"'

Good God, Archie thought, how Gobhlachan would puke at the notion of it all.

But to arms they went, nevertheless, despite the comedy vomit from Hah. Every man and woman to their chosen or assigned tasks.

'Well, it's not Auschwitz,' they muttered to each other, as they stood in the queue waiting for the jobs to be portioned out.

'My family need the money,' said Big Akiba the Ethiopian.

'My daughter has cerebral palsy,' said Janek the Pole.

'Better than working up that dingy pub in Oban,' said Hamish the Glaswegian.

'The lights must stay on,' said Sadie the Londoner.

'Never again – never ever that poverty again,' someone said, standing behind in the queue.

'I'll get a packet, then retire,' muttered Archie.

'If these fucking environmentalists had seen the eight of us fucking freezing in our cots when we were small they would not be so fucking smart at condemning the oil industry,' someone said from the middle of the queue.

'I don't see them refusing a lift in the car,' added another voice.

'Or refusing to go on trains or boats or planes.'

'Or refusing to have central heating.'

'Or fridges.'

'Or tellies.'

'Or computers.'

'Don't they know where electricity comes from?'

The job, therefore, was necessary. Like running a hospital ward, someone needed to do it. Some overworked nurse needed to be there to bandage up the drunk when he came in at midnight on the Friday night all swearing and bleeding. Some hugely qualified doctor with a brain bigger than Mars needed to be there to make that exact incision, to bleed that precise drop of blood, when the aneurism flooded the cortex. Just as photographers needed to be there to record the precise moment when Churchill or Gorbachev or Nixon raised earth to heaven, or sank it right into hell. Just as Napoleon needed a poet (as well as a mistress) to soothe his fevered brow. Just as a videophone needed to be there when Saddam went slamming through the earth.

Oil itself, then, was a poem. Or a priest, or a prostitute, depending on your point of view. Utterly necessary. At the very least, useful and pleasurable. Oil. Incense oil. Fragrant oil. Oil of Extreme Unction. Oiling the wheels of industry. My head thou dost with oil anoint, and my cup overflows. I don't have any bread – only a handful of flour in a jar and a little oil in a jug. For this is what the Lord, the God of

Israel says: 'The jar of flour will not be used up and the jug of oil will not run dry until the day the Lord gives rain on the land.' Money is none of the wheels of trade: it is the oil which renders the motion of the wheels more smooth and easy. The poetry of oil, and oil as poetry.

Ted Hah himself was at the desk dishing out the jobs. Almost like jabbing a pin into the wall, Archie selected one marked 'Elevator Operator'. He had no notion what it meant. He just liked the sound of the words. And besides, it was in the sector clearly marked 'Unskilled'.

'Excellent choice!' Ted Hah said to him, smiling. 'One of the best jobs going. If I didn't have to be here, there and everywhere myself, it's exactly the job I would have chosen! All you do is press a button and the elevator goes up! And when you hear a *Ping!* – hey presto, you press the other button and *Hallelujah!* – the elevator comes down! Good luck,' he shouted as Archie was led off to his chosen task in the Great Venture.

The job was precisely as Ted Hah described it: Archie stood at the bottom of this huge elevator all day, pressing one button for it to ascend, another for it to descend. Worker after worker, all clad in hoods and helmets with what appeared to be oxygen tubes on their backs and anti-gravitational boots on their feet, climbed in endless streams into the elevator. Once the regulation one hundred and fifty were crammed in, Archie pressed the button – *Ping!* – and away the elevator went, up into the sky. After a while the *Ping!* sound would be heard and Archie would press the other button, and – *Ping!* – in would come one hundred and fifty different workers (at least he thought they were different workers – it was pretty hard to make out beneath all that gear) and stream back down the hill past the endless queue of workers waiting to ascend.

Archie had no notion where they ascended to or where they descended from. No one spoke, for they were all too busy working, ascending and descending.

Maybe they're going up to heaven, he thought idly, or digging a hole up there in the sky, rather than down there in the earth. Drilling upwards and not downwards. Maybe that's what all that stuff about north meant. All that stuff about there being no further north once you got to 90 per cent north, only south. Maybe they had to go up to go down. When there was no other way to go, folk would go up.

Maybe they were now actually drilling the heavens themselves. Making a hole in the curtain of the sky so that the very dewdrops of heaven could be harnessed. No wonder Ted Hah wished to call it The Oil of Gladness! But then again, maybe Hah was just mad. Completely mad. Bonkers A1. But what do I care? What does it really matter to me? thought Archie. I'm happy enough here, pressing this effing button and – *Ping!* – off they go up into the sky. And then pressing it again and – *Ping!* – back they come, right out of the sky.

That evening, after supper, Ted Hah asked him how he'd gotten on.

'Excellent,' said Archie, truthfully. 'I just did exactly as you said, and it was easy-peasy. Press and whoosh! *Ping!* – up the elevator goes! And press and whoosh! *Ping!* – back down it comes!' He paused. 'Bit boring, though.'

Ted Hah smiled. 'I know, I know. Sorry, but that's life. Can't always be songs and roses. Sometimes it just has to be done. The less we know about how sausages are made, the better. As Otto von Bismarck once said, "I am bored; the great things are done. The German Reich is made." Sometimes the boring jobs have to be done. Press pull off on up down in out… that kind of thing. Necessary though. In fact, essential.

Critical. We can't all be Caesars, crossing Rubicons and making grand speeches for posterity. Somebody needs to sit on the sidewalk to applaud the princess as she goes by. Where there's real work to be done, son, that's when we need real workers like you. Those who can stand and wait. Those not seeking any glory for themselves. The button-pushers. The diggers. The shovellers.

'And remember this,' he said, drawing himself up to his full six feet, 'without you, the whole operation would crumble tomorrow. For want of a nail. That kind of stuff. You know the rest.'

'But a machine could do it,' protested Archie. 'Surely it could be mechanised – computerised?'

'It could – of course it could,' replied Ted Hah. 'But that's not what the ascending and descending men want. Or need. What they need at that critical point of entry and exit is a human face, not a machine. What they need to see before they depart into the skies is the last sight of a real, warm, living human face. To reassure them. And that's exactly what they also need on their return from the Great Journey – a real, warm, living human face to welcome them back to earth. It may seem just like pressing two buttons to you, son, but in reality it's the difference between life and death.' He drew nearer Archie. '*Ping!* is the difference between production and nothingness.' He was now intimately close to him. 'In fact, Archibald Grierson, you are the difference – *Ping!* – between heaven and hell.'

Archie really wanted to ask something, but was afraid. Where actually do they go to up there in the sky? What are they at? What do they do? These questions seemed so simple as to be foolish. Surely everyone must know already. It must be obvious. Everyone else must just have worked it out. Why was he so stupid? Besides, you simply never just asked the giant – 'Hey you, you big lump, what have you got there, up at the top of that beanstalk?'

Because you knew fine what he had right up there at the top of the beanstalk: gold! Unless, of course, it was all a diversion and this was just a false tree, a false move, a false sky and the real tree and the real gold was elsewhere, hidden away where you least expected it, right in front of your eyes. Was it all a sham? A charade?And Archie remembered that great story of the emperor's new clothing, and the whole universe applauding nothing. Maybe that's what Ted Hah himself meant by that intense phrase he'd used a moment ago, when he'd stared right into his eyes and said: production and nothingness.

Were these really the alternatives? Extracting every last ounce out of the earth, out of Angelina and Brawn and John the Goblin, out of whoever – or nothingness? Archie had cut enough seaweed and stoked Gobhlachan's peat fire long enough to know that was a lie. You never cut all the seaweed. You never took all the fish. You never burnt the last peat. You never told the final story. No potatoes grew out of unfurrowed ground. Calves died without milk. The Irish starved without food. A people without vision perish.

So he asked the question: 'What are they doing up there in the sky?'

'Have you never heard the song?' Ted Hah replied, in his singsong southern-eastern, Texan-Chinese, clipped drawl, and he sang in a high falsetto voice:

> '*"Forward, the Light Brigade!"*
> *Was there a man dismayed?*
> *Not though the soldiers knew*
> *Someone had blundered:*
> *Theirs not to make reply,*

Theirs not to reason why,
Theirs but to do and die:
Into the valley of Death
Rode the six hundred.'

'You mean you don't know?' Archie asked, and Ted looked mournful, as that emperor must have looked that bright morning when the small boy shouted 'Naked!'.

'No one knows,' he replied. 'At least, not here. We just do our jobs. And fine jobs they are too.' But then he brightened. 'But likely they'll know at HQ. Yes,' he said, brightening even further. 'Yes, of course they'll know there.'

'And where is this HQ?' Archie asked, now actually feeling some pity for poor old Ted Hah. All soundbites and bluster, all hot air and paper.

'Oh – everywhere,' said Ted, clearly and simply. 'They have branches everywhere – Taiwan, Washington, Rio, London, Stockholm – you name it. I've been there, of course,' he said, smiling. 'Been to them all. Once you get to my level you do get some special treatment. Beautiful cities. Beautiful galleries. Beautiful women. You've already seen some of them here – I believe Barbara the San Franciscan gave you your croissants this morning, no?'

'Yes,' said Archie. 'She was lovely. And the croissants were excellent.'

'Oh, I'm glad you think so – we have them specially flown in from Paris overnight, every night.' He looked at his watch. 'Anyway, son, this won't bring the peats home – that's what they'd say in your own country, eh?'

Archie laughed.

'Yep,' he agreed, 'that's certainly what they would say in my own country – this won't bring the peats home.' And he returned to his air-conditioned room to rest for the rigours of the next day, pressing more – well, actually, the same – buttons.

Brawn was happy too, having also been given an outdoor job, though much more strenuous than Archie's. Instead of pressing any buttons, Brawn was part of the team which physically hauled the elevator up into the sky through a complicated system of ropes and harnesses and pulleys and weights and counterweights. To the unskilled observer the job might have appeared all brawn and no brain, but actually it required tremendous dexterity, ingenuity and judgment as well as courage and strength.

It wasn't merely a matter of dragging and hauling like an ox with a plough, but a job which involved the essential complexities of hydraulic engineering and physics alongside the necessary mathematical calculations. You could hardly just kick a horse and hope he'd head off and bring the peats home for you. You had to nurture him. Become the horse whisperer, the one who could smooth down the fevered flank. The elevator and harnesses were rather like the machinery you see on ski slopes, all wheels and gauges and flanges, except that here in the frozen north eternal vigilance was required to keep the wheels smoothly turning along the frozen wires.

Brawn's basic job was to keep an eye on the permafrost, to judge where the fatal sticking point might next appear. It required a sharp eye and alacrity and then courage and strength to leap up and unshackle the moving wires from the frost which threatened the constant movement of the elevator up into the sky. More often than not it involved Brawn and his compatriots physically holding the elevator, with the one hundred and fifty workers inside, at bay, while they hacked and tore at the frost which threatened to put the whole operation in jeopardy. Brawn soon took on heroic proportions for his willingness to climb higher, reach out further and move heavier weights than anyone they'd ever known. In fact, because of his speed at reacting to things, his co-workers took to calling him Brains. Maybe it was the permafrost, but he'd given up both smoking and farting. And he never spoke, either brokenly or like liquid poetry. Archie began to call him Fionn.

Angelina and Jewel were instantly offered work as bunny-girls, but they refused, so they were cast into the deepest recesses of the pay-office to fill in endless ledgers about income and expenditure. This accountancy department was run by a Welsh girl, Tanya, who used to be features editor for *Cosmopolitan*.

'The same reason as everyone else – the money,' she said.

Surprisingly, they used typewriters instead of computers.

'Much more trustworthy,' Ted Hah whispered. 'Ribbons and fingers. New technology is always breaking down. The cables and USB ports hardly last minutes in these frozen wastes.'

Angelina and Jewel were placed at the back desks in the office, where they were engaged in registering all the details of the new workforce: date of birth, place of birth, marital status, insurance numbers and so forth. The full data was gathered somewhere, though no one was really sure where.

'Accuracy is what matters,' stressed Tanya. 'One tiny mistake in the numbers and the whole system falls apart. Profits tumble. Chaos ensues. Disaster follows. Unemployment, failure and poverty – the three enemies you don't want to be walking the road with.' She'd learned well enough to say it with a hint of sarcasm.

Angelina and Jewel bent to their work like schoolgirls, their tongues at the edge of their mouths, transferring numbers and names from one ledger to the other. Like Archie's work, it was more important than it looked.

'It's very like my work at *Cosmopolitan*,' Tanya said. 'Very much like writing – the craft is in the tiny details, not in the big themes. Sex, for instance: that was just an advert. What really sold was romance.'

Now and again Archie saw the others going about their daily tasks. He'd see Fionn every day, his huge shoulder to the elevator, but the rest of his friends were spread throughout the drilling camp. Sergio ended up peeling tatties at the back of the vast kitchen, where Archie occasionally caught sight of him through the regular circles he made in the frosted glass window. Peering through, they would put their noses together on each side of the freezing glass, mouthing unheard words at each other across the glazed universe.

Ludo had ended up as the personnel officer, housed in an eyrie of an office perched on thick oak beams high above the camp, from where he could see everyone in the whole world. He had a huge chart on his wall which was a perfect reflection of the actual site down below, with all the barracks and beds and sheds marked clearly in blue, and everyone's names and financial and insurance details equally clearly marked in red.

Like everyone else's job, it seemed easier than it really was. Ludo's experience in creating and operating phantom crews at sea was critical, for though everyone had names and jobs, the actual work they did, the tasks involved and their ultimate purpose were a complete mystery to him. But the thing he'd learned at sea was never to ask such unimportant questions: he was there to work efficiently and economically. Maybe they *were* saving the world. His job was to keep a precise documentation of who they were (or sometimes pretended to be), where precisely they slept, where precisely they worked, when precisely they started working and when precisely they finished working. That information, of course, was not used for any underhand or devious purpose – it was merely used to calculate how much time off was due, what their International National Insurance contributions should be, how much tax they should be paying, what Pension Bracket they should be in and so on and so forth.

Data was all.

Death was the difficult thing. For even in this chosen, remote community, and despite Angelina's miraculous recovery, people died. Daily, new pilgrims arrived. Daily, seeping away hour by hour, others dropped out, departing like Captain Oates into the snow, or hitching their rucksacks on their backs and heading south, or crowding on the back of sledges or jeeps, never to be seen again, or harnessing a horse and heading out into the blizzard, to be gone some time, or tying themselves to skis and moving off, like eagles out of the Brisote wind.

Meanwhile, like those endless convoys in *The Grapes of Wrath*, the arrivals would drift in out of the snow like ghosts of themselves, crouched and frostbitten. This human flood was what made things difficult for Ludo: how to count the number of waves washing on to the shore as well as keep an account of how much sea-water merged back with the invisible tide.

Ludo had to resort to fiction for accuracy. To make things balance, names had to be invented, arrivals exaggerated or understated, the disappeared underestimated, the sick-list minimised, the worker–production ratio embellished downwards or upwards, according to need or circumstance. He was a long expert at it and no one ever really noticed – or, for that matter, really cared – that his fiction was an even greater achievement than the reality.

Like everyone else in the drilling camp, Archie saw John

the Goblin when he went for his monthly haircut. Being semi-crippled, John the Goblin had been given a special assignment by Ted Hah: he was the camp barber. Sitting for ten hours a day in a specially designed thermal chair outside the Frozen Fingers Saloon, he dealt with fifty men a day, giving exactly ten minutes to each haircut. (The women had a hairdresser for themselves, a Cherokee girl called Akira, whose long black mane was the envy and desire of all).

The Goblin had a bowl which he stuck on the men's heads and shaved around. A 'Number 1' he called it. It was the only hairstyle he knew, though he went through the ritual of showing each client catalogues and brochures and pamphlets of differing hairstyles, ranging from the Tony Curtis – a pushed-back, bouffant-style wave at front – to the Silvio Berlusconi, a stylish but minimal cut 'for the balder pate', as the advert so boldly put it.

The leafing through the brochures, which was the most enjoyable part of the whole thing, took eight minutes. The haircut itself, two, including the taking off of the cape and the brushing up. Somehow, John the Goblin had managed to get himself a glass igloo, signposted 'Bertie the Barber', through which he and the customer could see outside, but which was frosted on the outside, and impossible to see into.

'Well, John, you've really landed on your feet here,' Archie ribbed him every time he came for his haircut. 'Your very own one-way glass igloo. Your very own thermal chair. And these tips too,' he added, nodding towards the tin champagne bucket by the door. 'How do you get away with it?'

'Barefaced bravado,' said John with all honesty. 'You just give people – sorry, customers – what they want. Which is something cheap and simple, but dressed up as something fancy and complicated. Surely you must know by now that's what business is all about? And even storytelling, when it comes down to it – as the great storyteller, Archie, you surely ought to know that!'

Archie nodded, looking down at Haircut Number 50 – the bin Laden Look.

'All hair and beard that one, Archie. I don't think it's for you, Sir. But take a look at Number 75. That might suit you better.'

It was the extended Berlusconi look: the Full Yul Brynner.

'Far too cold for that up here for that,' was all that Archie said.

'People just like to talk,' John the Goblin continued, keeping one eye on the clock, which now showed that four minutes had passed. 'Lots of them come in here who don't need a haircut at all. What, after all, is a month? Especially for a bald man. But in they troop, month after month, follically challenged or not, and sit right there, Sir, leafing through all these impossible alternatives. The Berlusconi, the bin Laden, the Brynner. We used to have one called the Bush. There's not much of a demand for it now. Or, for that matter, for the slick sleek look, the Blair. But this one's in big demand – the Barack. Look – Number 100,' he whispered into Archie's ear, 'though it's just exactly the same as the Number 1, Sir. Short back and sides.'

He pressed a lever on his chair and lowered himself down to whisper further into Archie's ear.

'The stories I've heard in here, Sir. You wouldn't believe half of them if I told you.' He re-pressed the lever, saying as he ascended, 'Which you won't, of course. Mum's the word. Discretion is my name. Discretion is my game. Like a confessional, what I hear in my clipper-chair never goes beyond these glass walls. Now what is it, Archie – the usual, is it? The Number 1?'

And down he plonked the soup bowl on Archie's head, revving the shaver round the uncovered parts, like a mower clipping the lawn. A bump here and a cut there and slap-bang-wallop, and Archie was done and dusted, brushed down and sprayed, like a horse leaving the harriers or a patient the theatre.

In all his time at the Great Northern Field, Archie never once set eyes on Gobhlachan or Olga or Yukon Joe. At first this worried him, but Ted Hah reassured him, saying that all three – like very many others – were on 'special missions' where invisibility was the key to success. Questioned further as to the nature of these special missions, Hah was suitably vague, trotting out a whole series of buzzwords which completely failed to impress Archie. He'd heard them all before, and knew their hollowness: 'integrated', 'exploratory', 'visionary' – a load of guff about how Gobhlachan and Olga and Yukon Joe and these nameless others were the pioneers, 'the first force' on whom the future of 'the civilised world' depended.

Gobhlachan! thought Archie. Gobhlachan, who can hardly move with that cold anvil stuck up his arse! And Yukon Joe, with his glass eye and a dark monocle over the other! And Olga, who'd never really gotten over the terrible loss of her best steed, Prushka, drowned that time crossing the ford in the great flood north of Benbecula!

Oh, they're a first force all right, Archie said to himself, but not in the way this bastard means.

And then one day Ted Hah brought in the video. It was at the monthly press conference. As usual, the world's press had been flown in to be briefed and debriefed about the latest progress in drilling through the top of the earth. All of them, from the *National Geographic* to CNN, from the *Stornoway Gazette* to Fox News. A monthly spree such as hadn't been seen since the time Nero caressed his violin.

'I'd like you to join us for today's press conference,' Ted had said to Archie. 'Plenty food and drink. Come on.'

The news conference was just as good as the food and wine itself: full of goodness: how they had already drilled down to the Terastration Layer at a depth of 5,000 metres; how the Oil of Gladness was already pouring not just from the wells of the earth but also from the springs of the sky.

'We have discovered a way,' declared Ted, 'of drawing the goodness which has been frozen beneath these northern soils for millennia out of the frozen earth, by means of nuclear-electronic-physics, into the skies, from which we then drain it by pipe down to our own wells. The technique – niuclofidophysics – is based on using a magnetic samarium mirror to extract the oil's rays, which we then – at the other end, in the upper ether – where the oxygen and gravitational rates are minimal, are able to re-constitute as oil before pouring it back down here to earth through our own anticoagulant pipes.' He glanced at Archie. 'That's why we have elevators, by the way.' Then Ted Hah paused, put on his sad face and added, 'But alongside that great and important news, I'm afraid I also have some bad news today.

'Some of our most treasured personnel – free, law-abiding citizens of various nations fully signed-up to the United Nations Charter on Human Rights – in the course of their duties, have been kidnapped, and are currently being held for ransom at an as-yet unidentified location.

'I am not at liberty to disclose the kidnapper's demands, but rest assured that the The Alaskan Oil Company Drilling Corporation, along with the full moral, and if needed military, force of the United States of America, Great Britain and all the Great Free Nations of the World,' (he'd now begun to talk in Capital Letters mode), 'Are and Will do Everything within their Power to Liberate these Workers.'

He then paused, going into lower case. 'Meantime,' he continued, 'the kidnappers have sent this video, which in the best interests of free speech we've decided to show to you representatives of freedom gathered here today.'

After some difficulty trying to get the video into the machine, he eventually pressed the button to reveal a grainy image of Gobhlachan, Olga and Yukon Joe sitting on the floor, clad in the inevitable orange suits, their mouths strapped, their hands over their heads and masked men with Kalashnikovs hovering over them. One of the masked men steps forward, roughly pushes Gobhlachan to his feet with the butt of his gun, tears off his mouth-tape, points the gun right at his brain and presses him to speak.

Obviously through that primeval fear which drowns all things at great moments of crisis, Gobhlachan reverts to his mother language, Gaelic, and begins to speak. Ted Hah and the assembled press corps look even more bemused than the Kalashnikov-bearing kidnappers crowding round Gobhlachan. The kidnappers gaze straight ahead: French. German, Italian, Swedish. Russian, they think. Not that it really matters: the message will reach its intended audience. It always does. Or never does, Archie couldn't quite remember which. Hah and the Press Corps and the few ordinary workers like Archie who've drifted in with nothing better to do, glance at each other. Only Archie is really transfixed, listening to his own language.

Gobhlachan is telling a story.

Well, what else would he do? It is the story of Hector and the Balloon – *Eachann agus am Ball-Sèididh.*

'*Aon fheasgar foghair*,' begins Gobhlachan, in a clear, strong voice...

One autumn afternoon, when there was a big squad reaping for his father, Hector saw nothing better to do than to start making a balloon of grey paper. His father had a married farm-servant on his farm, called Donald, who kept a cow. So Hector shaped his balloon like a cow, and made it in every way like Donald's cow, as regards legs, tail, and horns. Then he went behind a knoll and let the balloon away so that it would go past over the reapers.

One of them looked up and saw this lump coming, and shouted: 'Oh, lads! Lads! Look at the cow.'

They all stood up to gaze at the wonder.

'God save me!' said Donald. 'Isn't it like my own cow?'

'Indeed,' said one of the reapers, 'if it isn't your cow, it's the image of it.'

'May Providence protect us! The Isle of Skye was always famous for witchcraft, but we never heard of cows flying in the air before!'

Donald dropped his sickle and went off to see if his cloud was in the field. When he reached the field, there was neither cow nor stirk to be seen, for Hector had put Donald's cow out to the hill. Donald went on home. When he got home he found his wife busy at her housework. She stopped and looked at him.

'Aren't you home early on such a fine evening?'

'Oh, I stopped working anyway, whatever the others did.'

'Is there anything wrong?' his wife asked.

'Indeed there is,' said Donald. 'Our cow's flown off into the sky tonight.'

'What nonsense is this you've thought up?'

'Anything I say you call nonsense. If I'm taking nonsense, so is everyone else who saw her along with me.'

In the video the kidnappers moved their weight from one foot to the other. Around Archie the press corps were busy texting, phoning and laptopping. A few had already left. No doubt to wire. Deadlines, thought Archie absently. Gobhlachan continued, in his strong, even tone:

'Isn't the cow in the field where you left her this morning?' asked his wife.

'The cow is not in the field where I left her this morning,' replied Donald. 'At the speed I saw her going, she'll be in London by now.'

'I never heard of such a thing,' his wife said. 'You stay here indoors with the children while I go out and see if I can find her.'

'Go and see if you can find her then,' said Donald. 'You'll need to be pretty speedy if you're to see her, however. I don't want to see any more of her. You never believe anything you don't see yourself, unless some lying baggage or other comes around when you'll believe every word he or she says. Go along then, and find out for yourself.'

Donald's wife went off, paying no heed to him. She was walking to see if she could see the cow, and there wasn't a single cow or stirk in the field. Then a heavy mist came down, and who arrived at Donald's house but Hector.

'Are you alone?' he asked Donald.

'Yes.'

'Where's your wife?'

'She's gone where she needn't have troubled to go, to

see if she can find the cow. I'm sure you've heard about the cow already.'

'Indeed I have. It's a terrible business.'

'Well, I never heard of such a thing,' said Donald, 'and may it be long before I hear the like of it again as long as I keep my sight and hearing. It was bad enough to hear about, let alone to witness.'

'Indeed it was; the world is surely changing.'

'It certainly is; we never heard the like of this.'

'Well, a thick mist has come down,' said Hector, 'and you'd better go to look for your wife, or else if she starts flying off it will be worse for you than the cow was.'

'Providence protect me, I was never in such a fix. Will you stay in the house along with the children for a while?'

All the press corps had now gone, bored if not baffled by Gaelic. Only Ted Hah and Archie remained, Archie at the heart of the story, Ted Hah gazing at the screen as if it contained some secret clue. Gobhlachan continued, the gun still hanging at his head, but the kidnappers arm evidently tiring and the gun beginning to droop. Staring tight at the video lens as he continued his tale:

'So Donald went out and stood on the top of the mound, and began to shout for his wife,' Donald shouted, 'HO, ISABEL!' (and here the kidnappers stepped ever-so-slightly back) 'ARE YOU THERE, ISABEL? HO, ISABEL!'

The gloomy crags opposite him echoed back HO, ISABEL! as loud as himself.

'God help me with my wife lost and my cow in the sky and the night falling,' said Donald.

He went back to see if he could find anyone to send to look for his wife. When he got back his cow had come home by herself, and was standing at the door chewing her cud. Donald looked at her.

'Here you are, you witch,' he said, 'sniffling at the door, but by your nose you'll get no further inside. God between me and you!' he said, going past her into the house. His wife was sitting there, having already come home.

'The cow has come back,' she said.

'Let the cow come or go,' said Donald, 'but you keep away from her. Don't go near her.'

His wife did not dare go near the cow.

As soon as day dawned, Donald went over to the farm to see his master. He went into the byre where the servants were milking the cows. He asked them if his master had got up, and they said he had, and that he was in the big house.

'Hello,' said Corrie, the master. 'Is something wrong with you today that you've come here so early?'

'Yes, indeed there is,' said Donald.

'What's wrong?'

'Didn't my cow fly off into the sky last night? I'm sure you've heard about it now. I've come over to ask you to shoot her, if she can be shot – I don't know – if she can't be shot, we must think of some other way to destroy her.'

'Tut, tut,' said Corrie, 'you'd better put that nonsense out of your head. Go home and take care of the cow.'

'Take care of the cow!' replied Donald, angrily. 'Not another drop of that creature's milk will go into my children's mouths. I'll put an end to her at once. If lead won't kill her, something else will. She's not going to be flying over the world like that!'

When Corrie saw that nothing could put this idea out of Donald's head he said, 'Well, bring her over to the farm, and I'll give you another cow in exchange.'

'Well,' said Donald, 'that's very good of you; I don't know what she'll do for you, unless you fatten her and send her to Glasgow around Hallowe'en. That's if she can be fattened. I'm told that the people of Glasgow will eat anything. Likely they'll even eat the Evil One!'

So Corrie gave Donald as good a cow as he had in his fold in exchange for Donald's cow. And Donald believed ever afterwards that his own cow had flown in the sky!

At that point, the video did the usual sizzling and crackling and ceased in a blur of horizontal lines.

Ted Hah switched it off and he and Archie sat in the great silence.

'Well,' said Ted Hah, 'whadya make of that?'

Archie shrugged. ' Hard to say. Could mean anything. Could mean a thousand and one things.'

'But they're in danger,' said Hah, standing up. 'Mortal danger. These men holding them are animals. We all know that.' He walked towards Archie. 'Friend of yours, ain't he?' he asked nonchalantly.

'Yes, yes. A great friend of mine,' said Archie. 'Came here with me. We go back a long way.'

Ted Hah sat down beside Archie. Wearily, with a terrible sigh, as if all the world's burdens were on his shoulders.

'You know,' he said, 'it gets kind o' lonesome out here. Day after day, year after year, pushing the very limits. Hoping for that great strike. The oil of gladness! Huh!'

He laughed quietly – a warm, human laugh. A true lower-case laugh. 'I miss the wife and kids, son. I miss them like an ache wider than even that hole in the ozone layer. You know, sometimes I think it's actually the same hole. A great void. Hey, you probably think I'm going crazy,' he stood up again, 'because I'm not.'

He looked dolefully down at Archie.

'Right now I'm saner than I've ever been.'

He walked over to the window, from where you could see

the entire drilling-operation. 'Vermont is where we stayed at first. Pretty little town called Ashgrove. Bets are you'll have never heard of it. No one has. It's just one of those run-of-the-mill American towns. Millions of them. Or used to be.'

He slapped his hands together, laughing that natural lower-case smile again. 'May the Good Lord pity me, I'm already beginning to sound like that guy in the movie – what was his name again? Willy? Willy – that was his name! Willy Loman! "The world's an oyster, don't crack it open on a mattress," something like that.

'Oh, you shoulda seen us the day we married. Marion was as pretty as a summer's day. The proverbial polka-dot dress. The stamping white horses. The little flags on all the verandahs. A real American dream, not an imagined one. And the kids came along too – Good Lord, now that I think of it, we even called one of them Biff! His real name was Jeffrey. Then came Bill and beautiful little Lucy.'

The sun was shining though the window: that pale Arctic sun which is all light and no heat. Ted Hah was standing in the rays as if they had been distributed just for him for this moment. Archie had never noticed before how old he really was. His shoulders, which were always held back erect, now looked hunched and small. His thinning hair was almost invisible in the bright shafts. The lines on his face were etched like granite, all bends and folds and bumps and holes.

'Then it all fell apart, of course. Bush – I blame Bush, but then again, he was likely as much a victim as all the rest of us. The downturn in the economy, the car factory closing, people leaving, squeezing the last drop of gasoline into the tank.

'Marion left, taking the babies with her. Said there were no prospects in Ashgrove – no future, no decent schooling, no neighbourhood any more. Sounds pathetic, doesn't it?

The very word "neighbourhood". Now so uselessly old-fashioned. You must think I'm just a sad old man...'

'No, of course I don't,' Archie wanted to say. Except that he did think exactly that: a sad, self-pitying old man. 'You're no different from the rest of us, Mr Hah,' he managed instead. 'When it comes down it, aren't we all in the same boat? Even Mrs Hah – Marion, I mean.'

How little room there was for sentiment, and how dangerous it was too – sticky and cloying, gluing you down when you needed to be hard and agile to survive. Good Lord, he thought, what grand speeches we could all make.

He looked around at the sumptuous press room, hiding so much nothingness.

'Is that the reason for all this palaver then?' he asked, feeling like that little boy shouting 'naked'.

But Ted wasn't thrown. Instead he laughed.

'No no no. Don't be so daft... so stupidly romantic. We may have created typing pools and all that shit, but don't worry son, it really is all hard-headed business. We really are, beyond the pulleys and the elevators, digging right into the core of the earth, and up into the middle of the skies. Don't be deceived, lad: it really is all about power.

'Here are the facts, boy, and not the froth: 25 per cent of the world's undiscovered oil and gas reserves lie right here under the soles of our feet in the Arctic. That's 375 billion barrels of oil, which I know won't mean much to you till the last barrel runs out and you're there freezing or fighting over the last flicker from the last piece of wood in the world. It's 200 billion dollars a day's worth, but I won't screw your head in with all these statistics. Just believe me – it's real oil for real life or death, to power real cars and real industries back home, in all the pretty little Ashgroves of all the world, so they're no longer reduced to empty towns with torn billboards flapping in the wind.'

Quite the poet when he got going, was old Ted Hah.

'So what's the do with the elevators and the typing pool and all that facade then?' asked Archie. 'What's all that to do with extracting oil and hard cash and all that stuff?'

Ted laughed at him. 'After walking all that way across the globe, how can you be asking that question? Listen, son,' and he came back over from the window to sit beside Archie, 'the only Ashgroves we have left are the ones we create. Do you really think any of that exists any more – Marion, with her polka-dot dress and the knees-ups on the Saturday nights, and the apple pie and all that stuff? Gone with the wind, as a better woman than I said, boy. Who the hell do you think we're extracting oil for – some imaginary Marion in some imaginary town? Of course not. But it's the only thing that makes it bearable for any of us, including the ones you'll never see, sitting in their real boardrooms. They too must dream that it is all for a beautiful Marion somewhere, raising her kids as decent law-abiding citizens. Otherwise, our tears would melt even this frozen waste.'

Another spin, thought Archie. The story about the story. The dream about the dream.

Though he was unsure. Surely postmodernists weren't ruling the world. The bastards wouldn't really be that smart. Or if they did, they'd be far too hard-nosed to care about it. These guys know all about the American Dream and would be far too smart to get sucked into that particular myth.

'I don't believe you,' he said, but Ted Hah just looked straight at him.

'Oh – it's not for any romantic, mythic reasons, though. It's purely a monetary, financial decision. You see, field studies showed these guys that creating exactly the conditions we have here – the typing pool and the ancient elevators and the barber and the air-conditioned rooms and Forces Favourites and all the rest of it – was much more economically productive. In the grand scheme of things, the dream is a very small investment for the huge returns underground. You ought to go there sometime,' he said, standing up to leave.

Just as he was by the door he paused and turned.

'Oh, I almost completely forgot what your old pal was saying in that video. You must have understood him. He must have been asking for something.'

Archie was tempted to say that Gobhlachan was asking for a million dollars, or for Ted Hah himself to be exchanged with him, but instead, he just told the truth.

'No. He wasn't asking for anything. He was just telling a story.'

'A story?' said Ted Hah. 'What kind of story?'

'A story about a balloon,' said Archie. 'How Hector made a balloon in the shape of a cow, and then floated it across the sky.'

'So what was the message?' asked Ted Hah. 'What was the subtext?'

'Oh – just that things can change. Things can be transformed. A simple paper bag, for instance, can become a cow.'

'That you can build a new world out of fragments?' asked Ted. 'That we can survive on wind and air? On zero energy, son?'

And he opened the door and went out into the snow.

8

WITHIN TWENTY-FOUR HOURS, Gobhlachan and Olga and Yukon Joe were released by the kidnappers, dispatched downhill on a reindeer-driven sledge with a note attached to an the antler.

'Sorry, mistake,' the note said; with a handwritten scrawl on the other side saying, 'These three people are not of the earth, so we have decided to release them. But beware. We will be back for you real guys.'

It was unsigned.

Ted Hah and some of the others in senior personnel took Gobhlachan and Olga and Yukon Joe to the debriefing station, where they were given blankets, cocoa and some apple pie and some severe questioning by a tall thin man wearing sunglasses. Ted Hah had requested that Archie be brought in as interpreter, but despite all the sunglass-man's probing questions, all three didn't give much away.

'Where were you when you were kidnapped?' he asked.

'In the toilet,' all three of them answered (in separate sessions).

'Where did they take you?'

'Out into the snow?'

'What did they look like?'

'They looked like kidnappers.'

'What do you mean?'

'Well, they rushed in with balaclavas and guns and pushed us out.'

'Did they have beards?'

'Yes.'

'Terrorist beards?'

'No. Just little safe ones. Like grandfather's.'

'Did they say anything?'

'Nothing we could understand.'

'What did they wear?'

'Black things?'

'Did they smell?'

'Yes,' said Gobhlachan. 'They smelt of fire.' But this was only because all of his taste buds were completely destroyed over those years sitting next to a burning kiln.

'No,' said Olga, because they didn't smell of horses.

'Don't know,' said Yukon Joe, because he couldn't really decide which was the best answer.

The sunglassed man left none the wiser, but nevertheless content, for he had a full file.

Later on that night, however, Gobhlachan and Olga and Yukon Joe revealed all to Archie.

'They were fairies,' said Gobhlachan, 'who had travelled from the west on wisps of straw. The mistake we all made was to have left that west window open. I should have known better – that's always where the host comes from. They took us with them on the back of the straw and we travelled forever through the snow, until it turned green. Their balaclavas were made of the feathers of blackbirds and their guns out of the darkened bones of murderers. They were confused by our sacred language, which, as you know, has special words to remove the tar from feathers and the *smior* – the essence – out of the bones. They were like naked men before us...'

'And not a pretty sight,' added Olga.

'...unable to do anything to us, and of course when daylight came they had to release us, for their feathers began to moult and their guns to decay.'

Yukon Joe, with his glass eye and monocle, sagely agreed with Gobhlachan's version of events, adding only, 'The real miracle was that they never discovered my watch. You see, I'd hidden it behind my glass eye, and even though it glinted under their stare, I don't think they ever suspected. They must have thought it was just some kind of spectacular removable eye, valuable only to its owner. For a while I thought they were going to remove my eye to find the treasure that was behind it, but they didn't. On the other hand,' he added, buffing up the gold with a spit and his sleeve, 'they may already have had enough gold in that dark lair of theirs.'

From then on, it seemed like the beginning of the end of the story. Gobhlachan was the first to go, maybe actually frightened by the kidnappers, despite his long experience and his sacred language. One night, late on, just when the Arctic daylight was marrying the Arctic moonlight, he just picked up his anvil and left, the cold iron glinting beneath the infinite starry sky.

Jewel saw him, and followed, signalling with her arms that she would carry the anvil for him, which she duly did, across tundra and desert, over ocean and sea, through rivers and rapids, up mountains and down screes.

Angelina and Sergio followed her footsteps, crouching down to distinguish her footprints and the scratches of the trailing anvil from the millions of other marks in the depths of the forests or by the drying riverbeds.

'There it is,' they would exclaim when their probing

fingers finally detected the sharp indentation of the horn or the more rounded shape of the heel, and they would rise and follow the direction of the trail. 'This way.'

Yukon Joe accompanied them, forever flashing his pocket watch and asking, 'What time is it?', nevertheless always coming to their rescue by making all the native tribes across the world believe that he was willing to trade in his precious watch for a loaf of bread, or a jug of water, or a finnesko of wine; having managed to do the deal, then always making good his escape through the woods or trees, bearing Angelina under one arm and the anvil under the other, always following Jewel and Sergio's cosmic trail to Gobhlachan.

The others left together late one night, to see Ted Hah in his lonesome cabin on the edge of the drilling-camp. They found him sitting on an upturned log by the wood fire, melancholically drinking bourbon.

'Come on in. Come on away in,' he shouted, but Archie and Brawn and Ludo and John Goblin stood at the door first reciting the Hogmanay song: 'We've come tonight to this land to renew for you the year... Open the door and let us in...'

'Well, howdy, folks – this is a nice surprise,' said Ted Hah, rising to go over to the cabinet, where the crystal glasses sat beside a globe of the world. He took out four extra glasses and filled each one of them with bourbon.

'Cheers!' they all said together, and drank, solemnly and silently.

'Well,' said John the Goblin, 'that's it, then. Thanks very much for the work. I enjoyed it. And I made a profit too.' He smacked the back pocket of his trousers. Brawn and Ludo remained quiet.

'Well,' Archie said, 'it's always like this, isn't it? When it comes to the end, you never know what to say.'

'Nothing. Say nothing,' Ted said, 'because you've said it all already.' He came across to each of them, in turn, and shook their hands, firmly and warmly. 'But could you guys just do me one great favour before you go. You see, my grandmamma was from Scotland, and I have a very warm and distant memory of us all gathering round the fire at Hogmanay to sing the great farewell song. Would you sing it for me?'

And Brawn began, in that deep baritone voice of his, right out of the drilled centre of the earth, singing: 'Should auld acquaintance be forgot and never brought to mind, should auld acquaintance be forgot for the sake of auld lang syne.' And they all joined hands and moved in and out singing the great universal chorus: 'For auld lang syne, my dear, for auld lang syne, we'll tak' a cup o kindness yet, for the sake of auld lang syne.'

And they began to drift out of the house, Brawn followed by Archie, followed by John the Goblin and Ludo, for the great journey back home.

And what a journey it was! Palaces where silken girls brought sherbet, hostile cities, dirty villages; travelling at night, sleeping in snatches, and the fear that this was all folly. Down and down, down below the snow line they reached a watermill and met a preacher who told them that the hole above the North Pole was, in actual fact, a blessing and not a curse.

'Have you forgotten Jacob's story already? See – there's the ladder. Angels ascending and descending for all of you. All you have to do is jump on to the ladder. Anytime, anyplace. Don't you know the story of the Tower of Babel? Don't you know the story of Stephen, and how he looked up to heaven as they stoned him, where he saw the Son of Man standing at the right hand of God the Father? Can't you see,' said the preacher, 'that the hole is actually the door? Go back, like the leper, to tell about the beginning of wisdom.'

'All that was a long time ago,' said Archie. 'Of course, I've forgotten some of the details, and poor Gobhlachan and Olga and John the Goblin are now too long gone to verify the truth of it all.'

'So how and when did you actually get back home then?' he was asked.

And old Archie replied, 'As with all endings, it happened much quicker than any of us thought. Yukon Joe we left in Toronto. Brawn stopped off at Vladivostok on the way home. We dropped Ludo off at Marseilles, where we'd found him. We then had three wild nights of partying in London with Angelina and Sergio, where we left them and a beautiful Indian meal at the Ashoka in Glasgow with Jewel before returning back home.'

'And then? And then?' he was always asked.

'Ah, and then,' he would say, 'we all just got the ferry and the bus home – Gobhlachan sitting up there at the front, forever chatting to the driver. Olga forever staring out the window, just in case her horses turned up. And John the Goblin trying to cut some deals with the students up the back of the bus.'

'And you? What about you?' we would ask.

'Ah, me,' he would say, slowly. 'I came back as I left. Came off the bus at the end of the village, still carrying my battered brown suitcase, and walked right down through the village. "There he is!" you could hear them cry. "Archie! Old Archie! Well, would you believe it." And when I came back home it was all exactly as I left it. Believe it or not, Bella was still curled up there on the sofa, cutting her nails, one huge, hardened slice after another flying across the kitchen. And the son was still sitting there too, tapping the remote control, as if some mystery would suddenly illuminate itself on the screen.'

He lived to a ripe old age, did Archie. The north wind blew and never bothered him one little bit. The earth gave way, and the mountains fell into the heart of the sea, and all Archie said was, 'Well, I told you so. But you wouldn't believe me. Nor would you believe Gobhlachan or anyone else before me.'

Archie increasingly spent time with his old friends. On windless, moonlit nights, he could be heard talking to Gobhlachan down by the disused smithy, laughing above the sound of the hammer on the anvil. On warm spring nights, when Olga's horses could be heard neighing down on the machair, Archie could be seen astride a wooden pole clopping across the sand. On warm summer nights, when you passed the old well in the centre of the village, sometimes you would hear the whispering sound of voices – John the Goblin and Archie, cutting the next deal.

But those stormy winter nights when the huge wind comes howling straight down from the north were best. Then you could hear them all: Brawn's deep baritone voice, Ludo sailing after him, Jewel and Sergio and Angelina and Yukon Joe, and even Ted Hah, laughing, like a wind which can not be discovered, or covered, like a wind which would uproot the earth, were it not held down by gravity, or reason, or complete lack of faith and imagination.

And I departed from them and they gave me a wedge of butter on a flame and paper shoes and they sent me away with the bullet from a big gun on a long glassy road till they left me sitting here.

That's how I heard it. And I left them there.

Luath Press Limited

committed to publishing well written books worth reading

LUATH PRESS takes its name from Robert Burns, whose little collie Luath (*Gael.*, swift or nimble) tripped up Jean Armour at a wedding and gave him the chance to speak to the woman who was to be his wife and the abiding love of his life. Burns called one of the 'Twa Dogs' Luath after Cuchullin's hunting dog in Ossian's *Fingal*.
Luath Press was established in 1981 in the heart of Burns country, and is now based a few steps up the road from Burns' first lodgings on Edinburgh's Royal Mile. Luath offers you distinctive writing with a hint of unexpected pleasures.
Most bookshops in the UK, the US, Canada, Australia, New Zealand and parts of Europe, either carry our books in stock or can order them for you. To order direct from us, please send a £sterling cheque, postal order, international money order or your credit card details (number, address of cardholder and expiry date) to us at the address below. Please add post and packing as follows: UK – £1.00 per delivery address; overseas surface mail – £2.50 per delivery address; overseas airmail – £3.50 for the first book to each delivery address, plus £1.00 for each additional book by airmail to the same address. If your order is a gift, we will happily enclose your card or message at no extra charge.

ILLUSTRATION: IAN KELLAS

Luath Press Limited
543/2 Castlehill
The Royal Mile
Edinburgh EH1 2ND
Scotland
Telephone: +44 (0)131 225 4326 (24 hours)
Fax: +44 (0)131 225 4324
email: sales@luath. co.uk
Website: www. luath.co.uk